WARNING Before DESTRUCTION

INKED BY: Tene Anisa

Warning Before Destruction

Dedication

This book is dedicated to my mother, Sandol who was murdered in 2003. I know you are smiling down in me and your beautiful grandkids. Keep being our angel.

Acknowledgement

I'd like to take this time to thank and acknowledge my wonderful fiancé Tony Brown, who spent many nights sleeping on the couch with me while I was up all night writing. She pushed me daily and always supports me in all I do. Thanks to my soon to be Mother in law Rochelle who pushed me and sent in the right direction to make this dream come true. It was many days she came to be my security guard from the kids so I could get some writing done. Thanks to my kids Rahliyah, Kingston, and Khari for putting up with mommy when I am focused on writing. Mommy loves y'all so much. Special thanks to Diamante Publications for believing in me, and helping me make a dream I had come to reality. To my second mother who took me in and taught me many lessons, but most importantly taught me "if you don't stand for something you will fall for anything." Thanks to all my supporters and readers.

Warning Before Destruction

Letter to Readers

I hope to encourage those of you who gave their all to a person who took advantage of that. Also to encourage those of you that've been to the FEDS and thought that their life was on hold or over. I'm also here to encourage those mommies who had to serve time and leave their babies. I would also like to encourage those of you that were raised by parents on drugs and had to fend for themselves. I would also like to give a huge encouragement to all the single mommies who wanted to give up so bad because it is so hard. To encourage those who are motivated to break generational curse.

To encourage those who feel so alone because they have no biological family. Encourage those who have been raped. To encourage those who had to strip to provide and survive but never wanted to make it a career. To encourage those who hold hate and bitterness in their heart because their past. To encourage those who recognized the warning before being destroyed completely. Self love, lessons, and learning from mistakes Is what made me push so hard for better.

Learning to forgive people who took advantage of you, even though somethings may never be forgotten. "Let go!

and let God" was a saying I got well acquainted with. Once you let that hurt go, you will discover a totally different person

Prologue
A Star Was Born....

As I sit here, staring at the metal bars in front of me, my life begins to flash before my very eyes. No, I'm not speaking on some near-death experience. I was now property of the United States.   The shit that lead up to this played in my mind as if someone repeatedly pushed rewind. Where did I go wrong? How would I escape my demons?

By the time my twenties rolled around, I was headed for self-destruction. See, my life has always been bullshit from my birth to my adulthood. I was born on November 9th, 1987 to Sandal and Steven in Indianapolis. Sandal had four kids total but gave one up for adoption at the age of 12. Steven had four kids too, and I was the baby on both sides. My mother and father's relationship was rough. He would beat her as often as they got high together off crack. After years of physical and drug abuse she was finally done. She packed our shit up, we moved to Dayton Ohio and never looked back. This was the beginning of a never-ending cycle.

Chapter 1
The Big Split

Sandal was addicted to men and drugs, two of the common denominators my mother just couldn't shake. However, she was also a hard worker, and she kept a job, food in our mouths and a roof over our heads. She met Anthony whom she later married. Shit was sweet in the beginning, until the drug and physical abuse started again.

Like every city we moved to I had one best friend. Her name was Ebonee. She lived with her mother and brother. She had a big loving family who accepted me like I was their own. Her mom got me enrolled in cheerleading. Hot in the ass we both had boyfriends who played football for the team we cheered for called Dayton Flames. Many days I would spend time with her and her family to escape all the bullshit that was going on with Anthony and Sandal.

After too many black eyes my mother finally decided that enough was ENOUGH. Her breaking point came to clear sight when he held her down in the tub, violently punching her in the face, causing her nose to break. Just as she had done when leaving Steven, we packed up and moved to Columbus, Ohio. Like always, people came and went in my life due to always being on the go with Sandal. The move to Columbus, I lost all contact with Ebonee and her family. At this point Sandal's drug addiction had become bad. Though we wanted for nothing, there were times she'd pawn things with value to get high. She was a functioning druggie; she did get her Bachelor of Science Psychology during our stay in Ohio. There would be times she would disappear for days, leaving me to fend for myself.

One day her thirst for that high had gotten so real she ended up leaving me at her friend's house. Her friend had a man and the ways he would stare at me gave me chills. Leaving me alone with this old ass perv, Sandal and her friend went to get high and left me downstairs on the couch watching cartoons.

Shortly after they left, the creepy man came downstairs and started touching my vagina thru my pants. "What you are watching, baby girl?" He stared at me once more.

"Cartoons? Is my mother back yet?"

"Nah. Why don't you relax?" He made his way over to me, slowly joining me on the couch. "You're a pretty one." He eased closer.

"Tha-Thank you." My heart began to race, and the trembling started. I wanted to scream for help, but I had no idea what this man was capable of, nor did I want to find out. "Stop. Get off me!" I yelled.

His hands had made their way between my shaking legs. "Calm down, this is okay. You know this feels good to you. It's a good touch." He said still touching me. He finally stopped. "Don't move, I'll be right back." He demanded.

As I got up to run out the front door, Sandal and her friend were coming in.

"Whoa! Girl, I know you are not running in my house."

"Uh-uh. Don't be yelling at my child."

"Sandal, you better teach this girl some manners."

"Are you okay, baby?" my mother, barely able to understand me, asked. The drugs had a hold of her, there was no use in trying.

Scared of what the man might do to me, I said nothing about what had just occurred. In the car I told Sandal I did not want to go back over there ever again.

With her eyes bloodshot red and squinting to focus on the road, barely listening to me from her being so high, she said, "Okay, baby."

Warning Before Destruction

I will never forget that moment when she disappeared for three whole days. I had to take care of myself until she returned. When she did find her way home, it was evident she had been on a junkie binge.

"Where have you been, mom? You left me here for days!" I scolded her. Sometimes I felt as if she were the child and I had to step up as the adult.

"I was so high I felt like I was about to die, like my body was about to give up." She stammered between her words.

Summers, me and my sisters went to stay with Steven. He was on drugs and an alcoholic. Still maintaining, he owned a lawn company in his garage, and had a nice house in Indianapolis. He didn't play no games with us and beating our ass with the belt was something he did often. One summer he beat me so bad I called my mom to come pick me up and she did. Going from no structure to structure was hard to adjust to.

When I was ten, Sandal decided to give up on Ohio and move to Minnesota. We moved with her strange ass friend, Nakita. That is where I began to spiral out of control even more. I had my very first fight there. It was over a seat on the bus. My mouth has always been out of control.

"You moved my shit and it was in this seat," I told her, daring her to do something about it. My mouth was slick, and my hands were on point.

"I did, and what are you going to do about it?" she replied smartly.

I sat in the seat next to her the whole ride. When she got off the bus at the homeless shelter, I yelled out the window, "HOMELESS BITCH!"

I told Sandal about the argument, so she walked me to the bus stop the next day. The bus driver told my mom the girl wasn't on the bus. I walked to my seat, and out of nowhere the girl punched me. She got the best of me, but I fought back with everything in me.

I'll be damned if a few weeks later me and my mother were homeless. Nakita put us out because I fed her fish sunflower seeds and they died.

"Seriously? They were just fish, Kita. Where are we supposed to go?"

"Honestly, that is not of my concern, Sandal! That grown daughter of yours knew what she was doing."

I rolled my eyes at her accusations.

"See, that is the very reason that girl lit in on her ass on that bus, she has no regards or respect."

"And you don't have any fish," I teased at her spitefully.

"Get the hell out of my house!" she exclaimed.

I learned early that what goes around, comes around, and that thing called *Karma* had no limitations.

I wasn't worried after we were tossed out into the streets, Sandal always made shit happen. So after a few weeks of living in the homeless shelter we moved in with her friend, Stan. He and Sandal were just *good friends,* or whatever. She and I shared a room in the two-bedroom duplex. An older girl who lived upstairs from us by the name of Keundra introduced herself to me. Almost instantly she and I hit it off.

"You live upstairs right?" She smiled.

"Yeah, so?"

"Chill, lil' mama, I come in peace." She reached out her hand.

"Umm, nice to meet you, and I don't shake hands."

She humped her shoulders in agreeance. "I don't blame you; bitches are trifling and don't believe in washing their hands." She laughed hysterically, with me joining in on the seriousness of the joke. "My government is *Keundra,* but my friends and family know me by *KeKe.*"

"Nice. So, what is there to do around here?"

"I mean, there's lots of shit if you're into it."

She went on to tell me about certain spots where she had the best times of her life. Me and her began to hang tight. She was wild, and I was right there hanging with her staying out late, messing with niggas, and fighting more. Sandal was doing her own thing in the streets as well, so what I was doing was the least of her worries. I thought I was cute at the age of 12— thick, long hair, and kept my toes and nails done. My fan ponytail was forever slayed.

I lost Ebonee as a friend in Dayton, but I had a new bestie named Tracy in Minnesota. She lived with her mom, dad, and two brothers. She lived a good life. We met in school and have been tight ever since. She was calm, a good girl. Like Ebonee's family, Tracy's family took me in as their own. Many nights I stayed at her house while Sandal worked or was doing her thing.

My mama was about that life. I mean, after all the men she fought to stay alive, she was not scared of anybody. She instilled in me the boldness and confidence I have today. This was put to the test one day as KeKe and I chilled at the local neighborhood park. Why is it that there is always that one basic bitch who refuses to let us Boss Up Babes be great? She tried it and I'd be damned if I didn't finish it.

"What you are looking at?" Wondering why she was staring so hard; I focused my energy towards her.

"Shit." The salt came pouring out of this chick.

"Oh, I get it. You want to be my groupie?" Keke and I exploded into laughter.

"I want to fight you," she said walking up on me.

Of course, my instinct was to swing first. I was getting with her until I fell, and she sat on top of me yelling, "I'LL KILL YOU BITCH" threats that I never took lightly.

It was time to take control of the situation. The adrenaline rushing through me at this moment, which caused a vicious side of me to emerge. "Get the fuck off me!" I stabbed her in the eye with my fresh fill-in.

She got up instantly while everybody pulled her up. She walked her way and I walked mine. Searching around for KeKe's ass, I noticed that she had left me to stand on my own. *Bitches aren't shit!* I had to dead that friendship quick. Walking home, I realized my nail and the fake nail lifted completely, it was hanging on by its cuticle. I ran home to my mama yelling and crying.

"What happened!" Sandal was yelling over and over. "Girl, if you don't calm down and tell me what the hell is going on with you?"

"She ran up on me and we fought. I stabbed her in the eye with my nail to get her off of me," I told her crying and upset.

She went to grab her large dog chain she kept, looked at me and said, "Where she at?"

We left and walked around the neighborhood to see if we could find the girl. After a dead mission we were headed to the emergency room where they had to completely remove my fingernail. Sandal's drug habit was not getting any better, and neither was I. Once again, it was time to pack up and move, except this time we were parting ways. Sandal was at a point where she wanted to get help. She moved to a rehab in Florida, and I caught a train by myself back to Indianapolis. Once again, another bond I created with Tracy was broken from being back on the go.

Chapter 2
13 lost to 26

A house of six....

My oldest sister, Juanita on my mother's side, was my destination. She was 11 years older than me, and like our mother she was strung out too, but instead of receiving she was giving out the beatings, she was the abuser. She lived on the westside of Indianapolis in the hood called HaughVille. Juanita was married to her husband Eric for years, and she had two kids, which were by two different men. Living in the house was Juanita, Eric, her two kids, and our other brother John, and now me. Yep, six people in a two bedroom. I talked to Sandal weekly, but it had been a few years since I've spoken to Steven.

I was wearing other girl's clothes, my sister's clothes, and my brother's too big clothes. At this point my hair was all broken off from the ponytails. I was a dancer in a group called "Red Steppers"— that was the most involvement I had in an extracurricular activity. Making a name for myself, after the first semester, I was back to my fighting ways, and was introduced to sex.

I met a sexy, light skin, tall, handsome man named Jaheim. He lived around the corner from us in his own house, and I was walking to the corner store when he pulled up on me.

"What's up, little mama? How old are you?"

"Sixteen, and nothing. Headed to the store, What's up?" I said, blushing from this older, fine ass man noticing me. Lying about my age was nothing new.

"Your mommy and daddy let you walk alone like this?"

"Funny. I can take care of myself."

"I like that."

"Something tells me that's not the only thing you like."

He pulled over to the left side of the street. "Take my number, and let's meet up later." He was showing all pearly whites.

"Sounds good to me." I was switching my hot ass off, I nearly forgot what I came to this damn store for.

That night around 10PM, lying, I told Juanita I was going to my best-friend's house down the street.

"What friend you have got you coming to meet up with them at this time of night?"

"Stay out of my business, Juanita."

Jaheim met me at the corner, and I hopped in. There was no conversation, we were just riding and listening to the music. We pulled up to the house where I hopped out in my booty shorts and tank top, with my belly hanging out. He had a nice home where it was just him.

"So, you are living like this?" I observed.

"Have a seat, make yourself comfortable." He invited. "You drink or smoke, lil' lady?" Jahiem asked as if he were testing me.

Sitting shyly, I replied, "No."

After some pillow-talking he reached over to me and began kissing my neck, slowly caressing my little titties not even fully developed yet but just enough for him to grab a hold of, moving his hands down to unbutton my pants.

My body grew hot then cold. The heartbeat between my virgin legs began to grow as it throbbed. My panties became wet with unforeseen moisture. Before I knew it, his finger had made its way inside my tight, wet pussy.

"You scared?" he whispered in my ear, while still moving his finger in and out of me.

"I…" I let out a deep exhale. I have never felt nor endured something so painfully pleasurable.

"Talk to me, lil' lady." He passionately coerced me.

"No, just don't hurt me." I was nervous at the thought of this grown man fucking me, but I didn't let that stop me.

Climbing on top of me, he made various faces as he slowly entered me.

Letting out a loud gasp, he quickly pulled back just a little. He was so gentle with me.

"Mm." Faint sounds of pleasure escaped my lips.

Jahiem stroked in and out, suddenly pulling out after a few deep strokes, cuming all over my belly. I got up and went to wash my wet pussy only to find that there was more blood than anything. It happens. My virginity was taken from me at 13 to a 26-year-old stranger. I didn't tell Jaheim he took my virginity, nor did I tell him it was my first time though something in the back of my mind told me he sort of knew. Once I freshened up, he took me home. While riding and listening to the music, Keith Sweat's Right and Wrong Way flared through the sound system in his car.

You may be young but you're ready

(Ready to learn)

You're not a little girl. You're a Woman

Jaheim leaned over, singing to me while grabbing my chin. The affection he was showing me had me thinking he was my man. This man finessed the hell out of my young ass. Pulling back up to the corner store he told me to call him later. "Hey, lil' lady, call me later just to check in."

"Alright." Smiling like a Cheshire Cat I walked in the house, showered and passed out.

The reality of my cherry officially being popped set in the following days to come. We would talk on the phone for hours at a time or meet up at the park. An older bitch who just so happen to find out about me and Jahiem, like the sour apple bitter bitch she was, went and told Jaheim my real age, grade and what school I attended. She also told my sister I was messing with him.

Juanita wasn't concerned with what I was doing, but Jaheim cut me off like a bad habit.

Losing my virginity to that older man caused me to lose my damn mind, or as the elderly would say in the south, "Smelling Yourself". My bad attitude before had been mediocre compared to now. Me and Juanita would argue and fight often because I was grown in my head and it was times she wanted to tell me what to do. We fought often when she wanted me to babysit my niece and nephew which were not in my plans.

"You gone watch them tonight or no?"

"Juanita, these are your kids! I have a life too."

"A life? Girl, your ass has titty milk on that breathe of yours."

"Look, I'm not their mom, you are."

"Girl, I'll be back sooner than later, and make sure they are in the bed when I get home. Talking about your life." She would mumble while walking out the door.

I wanted to rip and run the streets. Not only was I fighting but fights in the streets became more and more of the norm for me. I also started having sex more and more. Finding myself falling more in the tracks of Sandal with her addiction to men and sex.

Juanita's husband, Eric, had five brothers. All which would come over often. One brother, Nathan, was 18, and had the biggest crush on me. We started to spend time together and sneaking around. Juanita would always make jokes about me and Nathan doing things we didn't have no business. I would laugh it off and keep quiet. Whenever we had a chance we were fucking— in the closet, the bathroom, including my room. It got so bad we would sneak away from family events and duck off. Nathan was a cool dude. He worked a decent job and sold drugs. My time at Juanita's house came to an end soon, as well as the time between Nathan and me.

The summer before my 8th grade year, my sister, Sydney on my dad's side, graduated from high school down in Atlanta. Sydney and our other sister Shawna had the same mother and father, yet there was no sisterly bond.

Chapter 3
A fresh Start

I hadn't talked to my dad in a few months, but I would be spending some time at his house. He arranged for me to ride with his niece, Cheryl. He didn't make the trip, saying that his back couldn't handle that long car ride, but we all knew he just wanted to stay home and get high.

Pulling up to pick me up, Cheryl could tell from the looks of me I was going through it. She got out of the car as I walked out of the house, gave me a hug and took my bags. "It's been so long since I've seen you."

By this time the emotions in me rarely showed themselves.

The last time she saw me, I was a baby. Cheryl was a successful black woman, independent, no kids, and she worked at SBC Global for about 9 years. She loved the finer things in life and worked hard to get whatever it was she wanted. She was a very attractive, slim, chocolate woman with pretty white teeth and hair in a bomb ass bob. Cheryl had a bossy attitude, but she paid the cost to be the boss.

When she picked me up and noticed how much of a mess I was, she began to question me to see what had been going on. The ride to Atlanta was 8 hours. It was me, her friend and son. I just rode and slept the whole ride. We arrived and I was excited to see my sisters. Hell, the last time we saw each other was that summer my dad put his hands on me, and I called my mama to come pick me up. They all could tell that I was under stress and something was wrong. I was all of 100 pounds, skinny, hair was a mess. I had a track stuck under my slick back ponytail, too big clothes and shoes. My teeth were gaped and all out of whack.

The Graduation....

The day of my sister's graduation came around. I got dressed but Cheryl and my sisters did not like what I had on. My oldest sister Shawna looked at me. "No, Rochelle, let me go find you something to wear from my closet and I will do your hair."

Yep, I felt like shit. They got me right, I must admit, which boosted my ego. My sister did my hair and got me a cute outfit. We attended my sister's graduation. It was a nice celebration. Before long, I knew it, time had ended in Atlanta and it was time for me to head back to hell, Indianapolis. At least that is what I thought. I cried like a big baby when it was time to leave. Cheryl, Sydney, Shawna, and their mama all held me close as I cried.

"My life back in Indianapolis is hell. It's too many people in one house, my sister Juanita is on drugs bad. All I'm left to do is babysit. Nobody loves me there. We don't have extra money for nothing. Juanita and Eric are always fighting. I hate it there. I just want to stay here with my sisters."

They held me as I literally broke down. This was not a stable living environment for such a young girl like myself. Sometimes I felt alone.

Cheryl looked at me with tears in her eyes. "We will figure it all out for you, calm down." She wiped my tears away.

We all gave hugs and kisses and hopped back on the highway. The next eight hours was just time to reflect on how much fun I had with my sisters and wondering why it was a necessity to send me back with Juanita.

As we arrived closer to Indianapolis Cheryl sat me down to clarify some things. "It's okay. You can come stay with me, understand?"

I felt a huge relief after hearing these words. At the time, Cheryl was living with her mother who we called *Mama Latifah*, her stepdad who we called *Baba* which meant father in Swahili, *Musa,* her two brothers and one sister. Her sister's name was *Patricia*. It was a nice big four-bedroom house with a spare room. They lived in the same house down the street from the house Steven lived in during the summer. When we were growing up, the Kwanzaa family had a perfect life, the complete opposite from me. They celebrated African traditions, so everyone had African names and celebrated Kwanzaa every year. They gave me an African name. *Tene* which means *born on Monday* and *Anisa* which means *pleasure* and *joy*. That name stuck with me.

"Hello?" Juanita answered the phone.

"Hey, I'm just calling to let you know we are still in Atlanta and will be back soon." I lied. "Okay, I'll see you when you get back." Her words slurred. She was high as usual.

The next morning Cheryl called to tell Juanita she was taking me in. It led to an argument.

"Who died and made you our mother? Bring my sister home now."

"For what, Nita? This child nearly had a nervous breakdown when we tried to bring her back there."

"Yawl fucking with my benefits!"

"Maybe you should get some help and stop using your own sister for a check!" Cheryl was not about to go back and forth with Juanita. My sister had more thoughts of losing half of her assistance without me in the house than my wellbeing.

Juanita's drug habit became worse. She sold almost everything in the house to get high, lost her husband and kids. Eric put her out and took their son. She sent her daughter to live in Ohio with her grandmother. Juanita was homeless on the streets, turning tricks, and getting high. John got locked up which was normal. He just got out from serving an eight-year bid. Within the blink of an eye everything was lost. Life changed for us. Some for the better and some for the worse.

It had been a few months since I talked to Sandal. There wasn't a day that went by I didn't wonder what she was doing in Florida and how she was. Steven was very upset that I did not want to come and live with him, but that was something I was sure I didn't want to do.

Cheryl began to get me together. I was at the beauty shop biweekly, my weight was picking up, braces were now on my teeth, and she brought me new clothes. Me and her sister Patricia became close. She was two years older than me, in high school, and I was in middle school. With her being older, it enabled her to have a little bit of freedom. Going from no structure to the strict rules of structure was something to adjust to. During My 8th grade year, my grades were still bad, my attitude was

Warning Before Destruction

still uncontrollable, I was still a hot ass, but wasn't
having sex. Cheryl was not going for that. She put me on
birth control.

8th grade graduation, Steven showed up. He was
trying to do better about being in my life. Sandal had got
into some trouble in Florida surrounding theft of some
money and now she was wanted by the police. She
hopped on the next flight to Denver, Colorado to stay
with her brother, Aldray and his family. That didn't last
long before he put her out. Sandal was still wild and had
her addictions. Uncle Aldray was not allowing her to run
as she wanted and have company as she wanted. She
moved out of his house and into her own place. She was
trying to finish her degree in education and was
employed by the Denver Public School. She was working
on getting her life right. She was always a functioning
crackhead. It had been months and months since I talked
to her. On the other hand, things in my life seemed to
always take a turn in a very familiar direction.

Me and Patricia were both hot in the ass. We started
double dating and hanging out. Times we would stay out
and try to sneak home. If ever we got caught, she would
tell the lie and I'd just agree. I for some reason, just
wouldn't lie. We almost ran the phone bill up calling our
boyfriends.

Warning Before Destruction

Cheryl finally moved us out of her mother's home and into a nice 3-bedroom apartment. I never had the luxury of having a queen size bed, my own room, tv, and got to design it how I wanted. Now a freshman in high school, my life upgraded so fast. Cheryl met a man named Brian. He was a boss that matched her independence, was very handsome, smooth, a graduated dope boy and drug user. The bond they had was tight. He had kids. Later his two youngest kids moved in with us. I was slick upset. Just as I begin to get spoiled, here comes two more mouths to feed and needs to meet. I had no desire to share anything with them. Brian's son, Ronny was a little bad ass. He stayed getting whippings for doing shit like stealing and acting up in school.

One day on my way to color guard practice, Cheryl's little cousin came out and said, "Ronny touched my vagina." It was sick. Brian found that out and he beat the brakes off that boy. After a year-long lease Brian and Cheryl split. He and his kids moved out while me and Cheryl stuck to the same school and work routine. Even though Brian and Cheryl parted ways they remained good friends, and he was a father figure in my life. The spoiling returned; it was back to just us two.

First real Love...

Warning Before Destruction

I was proud of myself. I made it to high school with no kids. It had been a minute since I've had sex. My freshmen year I was kind of known. My boyfriend was a popular baseball player named Tommy. He was the very first boy who wanted me, who showed me love, who showed me what a real boyfriend was like. We had real puppy love. He lived with his father and stepmom but had a lot of freedom to do what he wanted to do. His family loved me, and my family loved him. His house was the freedom house, so whenever we wanted to get nasty, we would go to his house. Cheryl wasn't having it unless I snuck him over.

One day she was in my room while I was gone. When I came home, she greeted me at the door, holding his draws. "I know you ain't been fucking in my house!"

Lost on how she found them I replied, "No, I was doing his laundry and they must have gotten under my bed."

"TENE! YOU KNOW I'M NOT HAVING NONE OF THAT IN MY HOUSE!" she yelled. I tried to convince her of my story. She finally let it go.

Then came the big scare. We thought I was pregnant. Cheryl took me off birth control because it was blowing me up and making me bleed for weeks at a time. I had to tell her to make sure things got handled the correct way.

My communication was not good. When it was something deep, I'd always write a letter. I wrote a letter to Cheryl letting her know what was going on.

Dear Mom,

I hope you will support me in this time of need verses punishing me. I think I may be pregnant by Tommy. I hope you are not mad at me."

I laid it on her bed and took a nap. She came home banging on my room door, we had a talk and she was upset with me. "Tene? What is this?"

"I'm sorry, Mom."

"Girl." She sat on the side of my bed. "What have I told you about these boys and your education?"

She went on to talk some sense into me, later placing me on punishment from seeing him for a few weeks. I had my phone so of course we were sneaking on the phone daily and seeing each other in school. She went to buy me two pregnancy tests which both came back negative.

My attitude was getting a little better, and I was now an honor student. Cheryl's main rule was do good in school, do your chores and you can do what you want. Couldn't argue with that, not even if I wanted to.

Chapter 4
Death of A loved Stranger

Steven was doing better calling and checking on me at this point. It wasn't daily but often. He wouldn't come over but always made sure he called me. March 7, 2003 I was fresh home from school, sitting on my bed, doing my homework, which was my daily routine when I got home from school. The door opened. I didn't budge, knowing it was Cheryl getting in from work. When I heard more than one voice, I realized somebody else was with her. I listened harder. It was Steven and Mama Latifah. I instantly got a funny feeling because Steven would call to check on me not come over. Steven and Cheryl's relationship had been a rocky one. He believed she only wanted to take me in for the benefits, so he kept his distance. He came to my room, sat on my bed and was talking to me with tears in his eyes. He took a long pause while looking at me.

"WHAT!" I yelled as more tears fell down his face.

"Your mom, your mother, Sandal..." he paused.

"WHATTTT!" I yelled again. I knew at this point it was all bad.

"She was killed. She died." He said softly.

At this point every emotion I have ever hidden inside came to life. "GODDDDDDDD! Mamaaa!" I bawled like a baby. I was so hurt that she was taken from me and I did not get a chance to say goodbye.

Mama Latifah and Cheryl ran up the steps as they heard me yelling and crying. I never thought the last time leaving Minnesota would be my last time seeing her. She promised me she would be back for me. How could she leave me like this? Why?

It had been years since I've seen or spoke to Juanita. Somehow everyone came together. Finally, after calming down, Cheryl told me she found Juanita and she wanted to see me. On the way to her house, Cheryl showed me the breaking news article. The article stated a neighbor complained of a bad smell in the apartment building she was living in, they called the police who went in and found 2 females laying both dead and badly decomposed, with a crazy murder scene of blood splatters all around the apartment. Reading that article hurt me to my soul because not only was my mother killed by a monster, but she left this world suffering, and the fact that I had not talked to her in a long time also made this harder. I felt like I was crying over a stranger which I loved.

We arrived at Juanita's house. She was pregnant with her third child, living with yet another man, still on drugs but at this point she was prostituting to support her habit. The house she lived in was livable, but it wasn't kept. The man she was living with and pregnant by was no better when it came to drug use. We sat and talked, cried, talked some more, and read the article together. John was locked up, but we reached out to the prison to let him know our mother was killed.

The final report was completed, only for us to learn that she was beaten and stabbed to death, and no one was in custody for it. Not only was it her but it was a friend of hers as well who was found in the house. Our first thought was more than likely it had something to do with drugs. She had to be cremated because her body was so badly decomposed. Once her body was shipped back to her hometown, Bloomington, it was time for the funeral. We stayed in a hotel because Sandal's family was very strange and funny acting. I always had an evil feeling towards them, from her mother to her brothers. Before we headed to the funeral, we met everyone at Sandal's mom's house, Elmira. Pictures of the murder scene was going around, but I couldn't look at them. Juanita and Uncle Aldray got into an argument because she felt if he didn't put her out this would not have happened. The funeral was hard. I felt like I never got closure because she had been cremated. I had a hard time processing things. I fell out at the funeral, lost it, missed school for weeks, had to receive counseling, and was angry. After a month of depression, things slowly started to process for me. John was not able to come to the funeral; he was hurt and angry. It had been so long since he seen her because he was locked up so much.

One thing that didn't change was the moving. Cheryl started getting $600 from my mother's death, but she continued to teach me to create a good work ethic. She taught me a lot about life, how to cook, how to clean, never get a credit card, and to never depend on anyone. I never had someone take the time to teach me things or the keys to survival. All my life I have been on the move. Cheryl always had dreams of living down south. She moved us to Louisville, Kentucky the first half of my sophomore year. We lived in a high-rise downtown. Cheryl loved the finer things in life and we always had a nice decked out house or apartment. She always had a nice car. We went back home to Indianapolis every weekend to get our hair done, or she went to get her toes and nails done. Her and Brian were still great friends.

I met a girl at my school, her name was Marie. She was from Tennessee, but her mother and father moved to Kentucky a few years prior. She had the perfect life. Both her parents had great jobs, they had nice cars, and a huge nice house. Her parents brought her a red Beetle car. She had everything a teenage girl coulddddddddddd doubt if she knew anything about a struggle. I was able to experience Tennessee State University's homecoming with her and her family. This was such a dope experience for me. I decided to attend TSU after graduating from high school. So, I applied. I was also able to experience my first cruise and airplane ride with them to Miami. It was a great experience. The joys of having rich friends. I made the best of each moment, all the while saying to myself, *I will never have fun like this again.*

Me and my first love, Ted, still talked often, but I had a boyfriend in Louisville. Boys were my downfall all the time. Maybe because that's what I was used to with Sandal, or maybe it was the lack of love I had growing up as a child. Cheryl still had a tight grip on me so me fucking slowed down, but it didn't stop.

Living in Louisville didn't last long. Before the second semester of my sophomore year we were back in Indy. All bonds that were made in Kentucky were cut short, like all other relationships with people I have met. I moved, met people, then move again and never speak to them again. I guess it's a part of life.

During my sophomore year, and first love's junior year, I was invited to prom with him. We clicked back up as soon as I moved back. Cheryl gave me permission to go. We wore ivory and killed it. I had the time of my life. After prom we went to his house and had a nice session to end the night. The next morning, he came to pick me up from home and we went to King's Island. His friend, Marvin, drove us while we rode in the back together. That was my first time smoking weed. After we spent a day at king's island we headed back home. On the ride home, which was two hours away, we had about three love-making sessions in the back of the truck while Marvin drove us. One session was so intense he was not able to control his erection. He pulled me closer to him, filling me up with his nut as he continuously fucked me. Within the next few weeks my period came, and we cheered as a sign of relief. I learned my lesson this time and waited before I said anything to Cheryl.

Me and Patricia were back on the scene together and running these Indianapolis streets. There were many under 21 clubs we could get into, and we made sure we did. Always being the center of attention for all the ass-shaking and line-dancing, we were cold with it. It was a club in Mooresville which is about 40 minutes away from our city. It was a city that black people had to be careful in because we were not wanted out there. Patricia had licenses and her parents gave her the van whenever we asked. That summer I was on a two-week punishment, I begged Cheryl to let me go out with Patricia.

"Mom, can I please go out with Patricia tonight? Please?" I begged and pleaded.

She looked at me and said, "Only because your grades are good and all your chores are done, but don't pull that mess again, Tene." Referring to what I did to get on punishment which was coming in the house past my curfew.

Chapter 5
Dating and Becoming the Star

That night, Patricia pulled up to get me. As always, we were on our City Girls fly shit and ready to go in this club and fuck it up. The ride there was our pregaming time, with the music on full blast. If we weren't there every weekend, it was at least every other weekend, so we became popular faces there. *T-shirt and My Panties* came on by Adina Howard, and we were grinding and moving our asses all around, pulling our shirts up to show our stomachs.

A dude who was about 6'2" with a football player's body came up behind me, grabbing my hips, causing me to grind and gyrate my ass all over his middle section. He bent down and whispered, "Damn, you going to call me later?"

"Sure will." With Patricia's phone in my hand I put his number in. We continued to grind all over each other until the lights came on and it was time to go. I texted dude the whole way home from Patricia's and was hoping I could get mine back soon from being on punishment. I told him my phone was broken but I would call his phone within the next couple days.

His name was Antwan. He was a popular senior football player at Lawrence Central High School. His mom and dad both had great jobs at Roche and Eli Lilly. They had a huge house in Geist, which was known for all the rich white people. They lived next door to Mike Epp's parents and was tight with them as well. Antwan had a job at UPS making good money himself, and he had a car of his own.

A few days later I was able to get my phone back. I called Antwan to let him know I got my phone back, and this was my number. "What's up sexy?" I said as he picked up.

Grinning over the phone he replied, "Shit, just got off. What's up with you?"

"Nothing, I just wanted you to have my cell number now that I have a new phone. What you got planned tonight? Can we link up?" I asked, letting him know I was thirsty to chill with him.

"Shit, after I hop out the box we can link up. Coo?" he asked me.

"Yes, baby, I'll be waiting on you." I replied.

That night he came to pick me up, but of course it was a double date so Patricia came and he brought his friend, Ronald. He was a rich kid too— lived around the corner from Antwan. His parents were out of town. It was a pool table and dart board in the basement. We all chilled, listened to music, played the game, and of course me and Patricia shook a little ass. It was a nice time. Ronald and Patricia went upstairs while me and Antwan chilled in the basement. He made me feel good, holding me from behind and showing me how to shoot pool. We had a nice conversation and cuddles. His touch felt so damn good. I didn't want this night to end. Holding me like this made me feel a way. Patricia went upstairs and of course she gave up that ass.

We snuck in about 7:00AM, and sat and talked about what happened, then we passed out.

Me and Antwan began to get close. He graduated the summer we met, and I went to the same school he'd just graduated from. He had a sister named Stephanie, we were the same age and she went to the same school. The first time I went to his parents' house his mom, sister and her best friend were hiding at the top of the stairs, I guess to see what I looked like. We walked in, they ran and giggled. I followed him through the house to the huge basement. It was set up like a theater, and the back room to the basement was like an exercise room. We chilled and watched TV, still no sex, but sooner than later I was going to get it. My curfew was 2:00AM. We set our alarm and fell asleep. We got in his red car, turned up the bangs and rode through the backwoods to drop me off. I went in the house and passed out.

August 4th was Antwan's birthday. We went out to eat and to his house afterward. We always went to his house and stayed in the basement. I bought him a birthday card that said, "Two things you are not getting for your birthday is sex and money," and I bought him an outfit. The card was a set up. I knew what I was doing. When we walked in the house I was greeted by his mom and dad; they both were sweet people. His mother was asking me questions and talking to me. Her name was Marsha and his father's name was Reggie. After meeting his parents, we went to the basement and chilled, making sure the TV was loud to drown out the noise.

After sitting there for a minute, I gave him some fire birthday head for about 30 minutes.

"You sure you know what to do with that?" He smiled intriguingly.

"Why don't you let me show you better than telling?" I grabbed his dick, wrapping my warm, wet tongue around his caramel shaft.

He hissed at the feeling of my throat expanding to devour all his inches. "Damn, it's like that lil' mama?"

"Shhh." I instructed him, as I gazed into his eyes. *Yeah, that's right, niggah, this dick is being tamed,* I repeated over and over inside my private thoughts.

43

"Fuck. Come here, baby." He pulled me up toward him. He began to caress my full titties, sucking on my neck. He slowly pulled my clothes off and laid me on the floor on our pallet.

I laid there as he intensively licked and slurped my pussy. "Oooouu! Mmy god! Mm mm, shit, daddy." I began to fuck his face with each stroke of his tongue.

"Go ahead and write my name all over this pretty pussy." He Whispered; mouth covered in my honey.

He came up and gently laid all 220 pounds on me and slowly slid his long and fully erect dick inside of me, five pumps and it was all over. I was a little upset that he came so quickly, but what's a woman to do when she's laced with A-1 pussy and a fire ass head game to match?

We laid there cuddled and passed out. As the norm I was home by my curfew.

Antwan had plans to attend Evansville College which was about 3 hours away. We kicked it so much that it was only right to make it official. I just couldn't see myself living life without him. All summer we had good sex, chilled with our families, and created a bond so tight. The relationship we had was great. He showed me love and his family showed me love too. The beginning of August it was time for him to leave for college. It was hard but he told me to do what I needed to do and when I graduated, he would be back to get me. Even though he was gone we still made sure we talked to each other and texted often. Whenever he came home to visit, I was right under him, whenever his mom went to visit him, I was right there.

It was the start of my junior year at Lawrence Central High School. The first day I was walking the hallway I heard my name. "Rochelle!" I kept walking because I didn't expect anyone to know me until I heard my name again "Rochelle!"

"Girl, what?" I looked back and there was this pretty, light skinned, long haired, brace-face, thick girl who was fresh to death. It was Antwan's sister, Stephanie. "Hey, Stephanie!" I noticed her when we first locked eyes.

"This is my morning spot if you want to meet us here every morning," she said as she was surrounded by her gang.

"Okay, sweet, I'll be back tomorrow morning. I have to get my schedule fixed." I could hear her clique asking her how'd she know me. They looked to be part of the In Crowd.

The next day I went to school, going straight to the meeting spot where Stephanie and her gang hanged.

"Heyyyyy, Rochelle!" Stephanie greeted me as I walked up. She was goofy and funny.

"Heyyyyyy, Stephanie and gang!"

Everybody was nice and said hello back. She introduced the circle. "These are The Bros, my besties Cheleste, Allison, and India."

Warning Before Destruction

The Bros was a group of dudes who were well respected around the halls of Lawrence Central High School and outside of the school too. Each bro was in a relationship with one of the girls. Quiet as they wanted to keep it, one of the bros was in a relationship with two of the girls but it was the best kept secret so there'd be no drama. Michael was in love with Stephanie and her friend Tanika. The gang was tight though, it was a brother/sisterhood thing going on. India really hung with us during school hours. We all became tighter and tighter, and soon I was a part of the posse. We were all known around the school.

Even though Stephanie was my boyfriend's sister she never told him what I did. Me and her began to hang tight outside of school. This was an advantage to me because when Antwan came home to visit from college, I would say I was staying with Stephanie. Antwan got a new car and gave Stephanie his old red car with the system in it. You couldn't tell us shit. Stephanie had a best friend named Cheleste who was a year older than us. She was in love with Tristen— they had a real high school sweetheart story. Cheleste had two abortions by the time they graduated high school, not to mention the many bitches he had her fighting, but she loved that nigga.

Let's talk about my first crush who was a Chocolate Adonis with a beautiful smile and nice body tone. His name was Lee. Lee was a popular football player who was a part of The Bros. Though he knew about my crush he also respected the fact that Antwan and I were an item. He used to have banging ass house parties. He lived right across the street from me. Party nights me and the girls would get ready at my house and mob across the street. It was a real old-school house party type of thing. Everybody was dancing, house was packed, everybody sweating, good music playing and no bullshit. He always had peaceful parties. The house parties started being such a big deal that he decided to rent different buildings to have his parties at. We were from the eastside of Indianapolis. Eastside doesn't go westside, and westside doesn't go eastside. Lee decided to try his luck and rent a building out west.

Our brothers had our back and we had our brothers' backs, so we mobbed out west. The night started off smooth, but as time went on more and more westside niggas came in. As soon as *Put Your Hood Up* by Lil Jon came on, the club got to rocking. It was a big brawl,,,,,, everybody was fighting from boys to girls. The fight was taken outside to the parking lot. We were right there with our brothers until the westside started popping trunks and pulling out guns.

"Everybody get in a line facing me and don't nobody move or I'm going to air this bitch out!" The westside nigga hollered. We all did as he told us. My heart was beating so fast. The parking lot cleared out immediately. "All you bitches to the car."

In silence we did just that. We hopped in the car and went to the back of the building. We slowly peaked around the building with the lights off to watch from a distance. The westside niggas robbed our brothers of their money, phones, and shoes. Everyone got in their cars and fled the scene. We took the opposite way to get on the same highway, where we could see The Bros car facing the opposite way of traffic. We pulled over to make sure everyone in the car was okay. They were shitty but no one was hurt. Once again them westside niggas was back at it, they tried to run them off the highway. At school that Monday it was the word of the day.

That was a brawl we couldn't tell our parents about. A few weeks later Lee was back at it, having another party out west in some apartment clubhouse. Westside got word we were back on their side of town and they showed up. See, our brothers were about throwing them hands so carrying guns was never a thing. Right after midnight all the bullshit began. Antwan was home for the weekend visiting and was on his way to the party. The westside niggas were outside with guns facing the door and would not let any out the building. Antwan came in and grabbed me and Stephanie up and took us home. He yelled at us for even going out west.

"Yo, tell me what the fuck were yawl thinking! These cats out west is not playing with you east bounders."

"Chill, big bro, we were good; the crew had our backs."

"Yeah, babe, we were fine."

"You? Shut up," he instructed me, then turned to his sister. "And you should know better, Steph!"

It was still the same bullshit with me, busting it open and fighting. Though I was always in bullshit, Cheryl had no way to find out because for all she knew, I was over Stephanie's house. If I did my chores and kept good grades, I could do whatever I wanted. Antwan was still telling me to hold on tight because as soon as I graduated, he was moving me with him to Evansville. In the meantime, I got my acceptance letter from TSU. As bad as I wanted to go to experience an HBCU I still wanted to be with my man. He started selling weed in Evansville and was of the biggest weed mans on the campus.

Even though me, Stephanie and Cheleste were tight, it was some unloyalty going on. Stephanie was madly in love with Tristen behind Cheleste's back. As soon as Cheleste and Tristen broke up, Stephanie began spending time with him, and I began spending time with his cousin. Everybody called him Yeller. It was strange crushing on him, and Stephanie knew, but she never told her brother. When Stephanie hung with Tristen, I would always go for the ride so if Cheleste called It wouldn't be suspicious. Cheleste and Tristen broke up but was still lightweight kicking it. Cheleste had a new nigga. A real ass street nigga who was getting money and very known on the east side. His name was Wheezy. He was a young fly nigga and he had Cheleste's nose wide open. She started to spend more and more time with his which gave Stephanie more time to spend with Tristen.

Me and Stephanie got jobs at the McDonald's inside the Children's Museum. Tristen's grandmother lived 5 minutes away. He called Stephanie's phone and invited us over, plus Yeller was there and wanted to spend time with me. Even though we all were spending time together, me and Stephanie never had sex in the same room until this day. It was 2 beds in the basement. They were on one bed while me and Yeller was in the other bed.

One thing I didn't do was put my mouth on no other nigga. Busting this pussy open was one thing, but that was for my man. Me and Yeller laid in the bed while I played with his limp dick and sucked on his neck as he played with my fat ass. Slowly but surely his dick started to wake, but it was very small. It wasn't even worth the cheat. I jacked him off and was ready to go. Hearing Stephanie's moans I knew what her and Tristen were doing. As soon as they were done it was time to go. We got in the car and talked about Yeller so bad while she talked about how good Tristen's dick was.

"Girl, I am not gone lie. That niggah, Tristen? He got that Dope Dick."

"What's Dope Dick?" I was curious to hear this shit.

"Bitch, it's when a niggah's dick is so good you can't help but to be addicted to it. Have a bitch out here feening like Jodeci." Stephanie laughed.

"Well, at least you managed to get your kitty wet, meanwhile zaddy limp dick got me feeling like a lost cause."

"Uh uh, girl, what? Did you just call Yeller *Zaddy limp dick*!"

"I said what I said, now let's just get back to work."

Stephanie's petty ass clowned me all that day. I mean I wanted to get my pussy wet. There is nothing worse than a nigga with a limp dick that is also small as hell. On the other hand, I'm glad my nut wasn't wasted on that fool. A short dick man could never! We went to work and finished our day out as normal.

Chapter 6
Senior Year

School was back in session. I made it to my senior year in high school, still alive and not pregnant. I was hoping this school year would go fast because I was still looking forward to moving to Evansville with my man. I spoke to Cheryl about it, hinting I was staying, and her thoughts were, "No, you are not moving there with him. You got accepted into Tennessee State University and you need to go there to get that experience of a historical black college." The good thing about this was, Antwan was still coming home every weekend and spending time with me.

There were a group of bitches who didn't like us for whatever reason. Maybe because we were labeled as the baddest bitches in the school, and our reputations proceeded us. They knew not to try us

Senior year we were still hanging tight with our brothers. There were a group of bitches who didn't like us for whatever reason. It was a few groups of mad bitches who couldn't stand us. Maybe because we were labeled as the baddest bitches in the school, and our reputations proceeded us. They knew not to try us

Cheleste was more wrapped up in Wheezy, and the new feeling he was giving her, that was less time she was spending with us. Whenever our brothers had a problem, they know calling us would get the issue resolved. One morning I was arriving around 1:45AM from Antwan's house I got a call from Lee.

"Where everybody at? This bitch over here thinks I am a joke!" He hollered as soon as I answered.

"I just got home. I can call the girls though and we can get it handled for you." I replied as I was texting Stephanie and Allison to tell them Lee had an issue we needed to solve.

They were already together so as soon as we hung up, about 25 minutes later they were pulling up. I went and checked in with Cheryl letting her know I was home from Antwan's house, and sat in my room until the girls called. When they called and said they were outside I snuck back out the front door. Stephanie parked her car in my driveway, and we walked down to Lee's house. When we got there, all the brothers were there and some off-brand bitches we never seen before. As we pulled up the girls had their brothers pulling up too. Like most of our fights it was never a one on one, it was always a huge brawl. Lee was pissed the bitch spilled Kool-Aid on his floor and didn't pick it up. The crowd walked from the doorway, down the driveway to meet the girls' brothers. Tristen was on the frontline as always, as the girl's brothers were lined up in the street.

Tristen was yelling, "MY MAMA AIN'T RAISE NO HOE, AND ANY OF YOU BITCHES OR NIGGAHS CAN GET THIS SMOKE!"

It was not his battle, but he didn't care, he was there on the frontline like he was. As he started walking toward the dudes, we followed. The main dude from the other team was walking up toward Tristen. When they finally met up, it all went downhill from there. Tristen had a hole in his heart, but that never stopped him from fighting. Him and dude met, and everyone else charged the other group. Tristen had a dude in the headlock, me and Stephanie ran up punching him. A female came and hit Tristen from behind. He left dude leaking on the ground, turned around and walked toward the girl, but before Tristen had her, Cheleste already ran up giving the bitch them ones. Her girl jumped in, and Stephanie was right behind her. I helped Stephanie just for the hell of it. We looked up and Tristen was walking around with a steel pole from a fence, ready to hit any opponent that was in his way. We heard a loud scream as the other people packed up and left. While we were handling the bitches, they started throwing rocks and hit Tristen in the chest. As he laid on the ground, we all ran to help him. My mama's cousin lived next door to us. She heard all the noise and came out. She went back in to get an asthma machine. After that he was cool. Him and Michael had a one on one moment with each other.

"Damn, bro, thought I lost you for a minute there. You straight?"

"Yeah. Takes more than some damn rocks to knock me off my game; you feel me?"

"Aright, can you stand?"

"Yeah, give me some leverage though."

Michael gave Tristen his shoulder to place all his weight on, helping him to stand on his own two feet. Both shedding tears and telling each other how much they loved each other and would never leave each other's side. They were brothers and blood couldn't have made them closer.

After the brawl I went home and passed out. I woke up to Cheryl banging on my door yelling, "TENE? GIRL WHAT IS THIS COUSIN TELLING ME YOU WERE OUT THERE FIGHTING AND CARRYING ON?"

I groaned, still damn near sleep. "I'll explain when I wake up."

"Girl, if you don't open this dang on door!"

I got up and did as she requested, jumping right back into my comfort zone.

Cheryl came to talk to me as soon as I rolled over. She wasn't mad I was out fighting; it was the sneaking out she had no approval for. So, like always I was on punishment. 3 weeks being on strict punishment was hard. Stephanie and Cheleste went to get tattoos. I was pissed them hoes left me.

Prom was coming up and I needed a date. Antwan already told me he was not going. So, I asked Lee to go with me. After getting Antwan's approval, he said yeah. We wore ivory. Everybody came to see us off, even Stephanie and her mom came to support me. Let's just say that was the worst prom date ever, the sendoff was the best part. The food was so nasty I spat it out in a napkin when he went to the bathroom. I never been slick or good at lying.

"So, you ate all that food?" He said as he came back to sit down at the table.

"Uhm, I ate most of it." I was smiling, but I knew he knew the truth that I threw it away.

As soon as we got to the place where prom was being held, we took pictures and that was the last time I saw him until it was the end of the night. I did not get one dance with my own prom date. He was a real bad sweater and dancer. He was out of his suit before I knew it. I was even more pissed because I toted his wet suit jacket around all night. The night finally came to an end and I must say I was more excited that it ended then when it started.

Cheleste became fake on us. She switched sides on us and started hanging out with the same bitches who couldn't stand us. Stephanie and I never thought we would see that coming but that's the funny thing about bonds and bridges— they can crumble at any given moment. Shit, you just got to be ready for it. My thoughts were she was mad because I came in the picture and took both of her best friends. We learned at a young age, friends and history meant nothing, and there is no limit a bitch will go to once they hate you. Our life kept going on, Cheleste did not stop shit. We were still the shit and known.

This was me and Antwan's second Christmas together. His family lived in Fort Wayne, which was about an hour and 45 minutes away. Cheryl and Marsha became cool. They both supported me and Antwan's relationship, so whenever I asked her anything, she had no hesitation to tell me yes you can. His whole family loved me from his grandparents to his sister in laws, to his little cousins. I mean I was the main and only girlfriend they were used to for the past 2 years. The bond was so tight that on Christmas I got my own gifts from everyone.

While in Evansville over the last two years, Antwan was slanging weed like crack. He had bows and bows of smoke; good smoke too. It was April, and in a few more months I would be graduating high school and moving to Evansville with my man, or so I thought, until I received a call from Marsha.

"Rochelle?" she said as soon as I answered the phone.

"Yes, Ma?" Calling her ma was nothing new.

"Antwan's house just got raided by the police, we have to hit the road. We are on the way to get you now so be ready."

"Okay, I will be at home waiting on yawl." My heart was in my stomach, as soon as I hung up the phone I called Cheryl to let her know what just happened.

Thank goodness it's Thursday and it would call for me to only miss two days of school. Cheryl was all about school, but she let me miss those days to go support my man. Antwan called about 20 times while we were on the road to make sure we were coming. Talking to him and hearing his voice reassured me. When we arrived at Evansville hours later, the house was a mess. Not only did the police tear it up but you could tell this was the bachelor pad with no woman to clean up. The police put his dog King in the impound and tore his house up from the top to the bottom to find whatever it was they could. Unfortunately, they did find the weed he had. We cleaned the house and packed it up. Antwan had his mind made up that he was going to fight the case from Indianapolis, and he was ready to come home. That made me happy. I didn't know what our next move was going to be, but I did know my man was coming back to Indy.

By the time we were done packing and cleaning the house he had a bond, so we went to get him right out. We all ate good, went to the house for him to get fresh, went to get some more weed, made a few money stops, and we headed back to the house. One thing for sure he was not going to let that stop his hustle. I love a street nigga. I could never figure out how he came from such a successful family, raised in the rich kids' neighborhood, but wanted to be a street boy so bad. We had to rest up for the road trip we had ahead of us in the morning. Me and Antwan laid in his room and had a great session. Afterward we laid there and had a well needed conversation before we passed out. He let me know how much he loved me, how much he needed me, how much he appreciated me, and letting me know he had plans for us soon. Antwan loved me and he showed it the best way he could being that we were only 18 and 19. He showed me a different love.

After weeks of fighting his case, he was put on probation which he got transferred home to complete. He smoked like a chimney and now that had been cut short. So, his new choice of drug was Lean which was Medicaid cough medicine. I hate him being on that because he would be so high, he would fall asleep anywhere.

One date night we went to dinner at Applebee's in Castleton, the rich people area. I'll be damned right after he ordered his food, he fell asleep sitting up at the table. I had to get our order to go. After minutes of trying to wake him up, we went home. I was excited my man moved home right in time for my graduation.

Stephanie had an older dude who she began to fall for. We called him DJ. He worked at a well-known urban fashion spot. We all knew, even Marsha, he was not worth shit, but that was who Stephanie chose to love, so all we could do was support her. He would drop her off at school every day and drive her car. Stephanie was loyal to her man, and that's what DJ loved about her the most.

He eventually got her to do whatever it was he told her to do.

In May, a few days before my graduation, it was time to break the bad news down to Cheryl about my final decision. I was not going away to Tennessee State University, I was staying home. "I am not going to Tennessee State University, Mama, I am going to stay home." I told her worried of her reply.

"Well, that's your choice, Tene. I will not support that decision at all. So, after you graduate you have to go."

Her reply hurt me. After the intense conversation I called Antwan and told him what happened. Quickly he replied, "Let me holler at my parents and I will let you know what the plan is."

May 26, 2006 was graduation, and even though I was pissed that Cheryl put me out and did not support me, it was a happy day. Steven came to support me, and to my surprise so did Sandal's mother, brother, sister, and her cousins. Her brother put a trust fund up for me for college. I did not know if he would still give me the money because of my decision to stay home. I still had plans to go to college, but it was Ivy Tech Community College. I guess that still was not good enough. After my graduation we all went to Mama Latifah's house. I had a good time and loved the support I had. Cheryl was so mad at me she didn't give me an open house party. The next day I packed my stuff up and left. Cheryl bought a blue Oldsmobile Cutlass Ciera my junior year from Marsha. She made a partial payment but when I decided to stay home, she did not finish paying off the car. Marsha had no problem with letting me keep the car without the rest of the payment. She accepted me and our decision.

Chapter 7
Grown Woman Shit

Marsha said it was okay for me to stay with them until me and Antwan figured things out. The money became an issue with me and Cheryl. Once I moved out, I called Social Security to advise them of the change of address. I still had a backdate check coming from them cutting me off because I turned 18, but I was still in high school. Cheryl felt like she was entitled to some of the money because it was her "child support". I was put out, so now I needed that to survive on top of nothing outside of the trust fund from Sandal's brother. I cannot give anything extra.

Within weeks the check was in the mailbox at Marsha's house. I was enrolled in Ivy Tech Community College like I said I was going to do. Cheleste and Reggie were on their first baby. However, me, her, and Stephanie were determined to make it through college. Stephanie's saying was, *"I can't have a baby until I'm riding rims."* Antwan told me to focus on getting through school and not to worry about a job. We finally decided we would get us a 2 bedroom and roommate with

Stephanie. She attended I.U.P.U.I. With her parents having good jobs she was able to go to a great college.

Me, Stephanie and Marsha began going out everyday apartment hunting for a 2-bedroom, 2-bathroom apartment. After a few weeks of searching, we finally found us a nice apartment on the northside of Indiana, close to our school and by a lot of stores.

We were finally settled in our new apartment nice and cozy. The bedrooms were dived by the living room, dining room and kitchen. So, we had our peace and quiet. We had the hang out spot. It was always filled with the aroma of weed from Antwan selling it and everybody around smoking it. He always kept a big chopper in the closet, once again mind-blowing to me because he was not raised as a hood nigga but wanted to be one so damn bad.

I was scared to try hardcore drugs because I saw how bad it took over Sandal, Juanita and Steven. Some people use generational curses to hinder them. See me, I like to use mine as a stepping stool and lesson of what not to do and try my hardest to break the curse. Smoking weed became my daily routine. One time me and Stephanie decided to smoke a blunt with Lean on it. That was my first and last time. We smoked that shit and was sleep for a full 24 hours. I see why Antwan would fall asleep.

Warning Before Destruction

Everybody was always at our house from Antwan's friends, our friends, to Cheleste who came over every time her and Wheezy got into an argument, which slowly but surely became often. Over the past years Wheezy had been putting Cheleste through some shit. Cheleste had to deal with bitches calling and explaining what the inside of her house looked like, shootouts, and many arguments with him and others, and a few evictions.

DJ moved in our apartment with Stephanie. After a while he quit his job at Devero's. From that point on shit begin to get rocky, even down to Stephanie finding out he had a baby on her. Regardless of her parents being set as far as financial wise, she always had a job. Around Christmas time me and Stephanie got a job at Steak-N-Shake in Castleton. Even though my only bill was my cell bill I wanted to have my own money. We made a killing, walking out with at least $100.00 a night.

Living together was working out fine. I was just always bitching because they treated me like a slave, always going behind them and company cleaning up. Other than that, it was peaceful for the most part. Working and school was my main focus. I felt like I had to prove Cheryl wrong, and still be successful. Me and her relationship was still rocky, and we went weeks without speaking to each other. One thing about me, I can hold a grudge and I could be very mean.

It had been a few months since I spoke to Steven. Me and Marsha's relationship began to get tighter and tighter. Since I did not get an open house or graduation party, she brought me and Stephanie front row seats to see Chris Brown. Antwan had a 2002 Chrysler Concorde, he upgraded his car and gave me the Chrysler Concorde.

Cheleste and Wheezy continued to thug it out. I can say she fought hard for her nigga and held him down through all the bullshit. The birth of their baby was coming up, and they were not prepared at all. Cheleste had to drop out of school to focus on her family. They had to move in with Wheezy's dad to make sure they had shelter for the arrival of the baby. That was rough too because Wheezy's sister and Cheleste started getting into it often. Cheleste would call daily venting about something that happened in that house.

Once we graduated from school, India started hanging around with us more. India and DJ did not get along. DJ felt India should not be allowed at our house because of the issues they had, Stephanie and India got into an argument and stopped talking to each other because Stephanie chose her man over her friend. However, India was still my friend and my nigga paid bills too, and he said he didn't have an issue with her coming over, plus she needed to vent, and as the good friend I was I made sure I was there for her to do so. We were all at the point of trying to get ahold of being in this adult world.

Stephanie was gone to school. India pulled up asking many times, "Where is DJ? I do not want no smoke with that punk."

"Girl, you are okay. Antwan said it was cool for you to come over. Now, come in, have a seat and talk to me." I said sitting next to her.

She began to vent to me about life. At this point we were all fresh out on our own trying to figure out the adult world. No later than 5 minutes into the conversation I heard the keys to the door.

"That's Antwan. He just texted me and said he was on his way." I told her.

Before she could get her next full sentence out the door busted open. "Why is this bitch here?" DJ yelled at the top of his lungs.

"Because she needed me, and Antwan said it was okay." I interrupted him.

India yelled back, "You are the bitch! You the nigga letting your woman take care of you. So, who is the real bitch?"

"I got something for your ass!" DJ yelled as he grabbed his phone from his pocket and walked out the door.

Me and India sat down and picked back up where we left off. Ten minutes after she continued to vent, she decided to go home.

"Well, I am sorry that crazy muthafucka came in. Just remember the words of encouragement I just gave you. Let me get my shoes and I will walk you to your car." I said getting up to get my shoes from my room.

As we walked down the hallway of the apartments outside to the parking lot, Stephanie stormed towards us yelling, "What the fuck is going on, Rochelle?"

"Get your nigga. He came in tripping 'cause India came here to talk to me!" I yelled back.

"Bitch, you know what the fuck is going on, and you know he has no sense. I do not know why the fuck you would even do that messy shit," Stephanie said.

"It only got messy because he made it messy," I said as me and India started walking toward her car.

When we got to the end of the hallway outside, we saw DJ standing out there as a group of niggas pulled up, turning in our apartment on two wheels. They all jumped out the car loud and looking for the issue. DJ's dumb ass called his niggas from his hood, Post Road, and with no hesitation they came running.

"Now what is the problem, bro?" The main leader hopped out and yelled.

"NOTHING! He called you all for a FEMALE. It's no problem so yawl can get back in yawl car and leave!" I yelled to make sure shit was understood. I knew DJ was fucked up mentally, but I never expected him to pull some hoe shit like this. We had many complaints from the office about our noise levels, so getting them out the complex was my main concern.

"A FEMALE?" His nigga looked a DJ and yelled, "My nigga you are tripping! We are out of here!"

"Yes, a little female at that!" I hollered to make sure all confusion was settled.

The Post Road gang left, and that was when Antwan pulled up. India got in her car and left. DJ and Stephanie went into the house.

After standing outside telling Antwan what happened, we walked in the house as Antwan was walking me behind me. A few feet from the doorway I could hear DJ and Stephanie arguing about the shit still. I was feeling bad for the way shit transpired, but I still felt like I needed to be there for my friend. See, all my life people have come and gone so when I get attached to someone and create a bond that is something I take seriously. India texted me a message telling me I am a good friend to her, but it will always be bullshit and she felt like we just needed to be friends from a distance. Once again, another bond was broken, and another lost.

Me and Stephanie had not talked in a few days. She was very mad at me. Once we did talk, I understood where she was coming from. Stephanie was always all about making her man happy. After our conversation we made up.

Cheryl called to "check on me" as she said but I think she just called to see if I had gotten my last check from Social Security. I got it a few weeks ago and just decided not to tell her. I gave Antwan $500.00, went shopping and put the rest of the money away. When Cheryl asked about the money I just lied and told her, "No, it still has not come." I really felt like she was not obligated to anymore of my money after putting me out like she did. Not only did I feel like that, but Marsha and Antwan felt the same way and they stayed on me to not give any of my money away.

Chapter 8
The Bullshit

I have always been a no tolerance type of person. It may have something to do with how I grew up, but I was not for it. I also held grudges so once you fuck me over, I will not be the first to apologize. I was no longer working at Steak-N-Shake. Between taking odds from Antwan's pockets, the money he knowingly gave me, and selling little sacks of his weed, I was straight, and working was not for me. Antwan was still on Lean, but now that he was off probation in Evansville, he was lacing his blunts with Lean.

For the third time Antwan did not make it home. I stayed up all night calling his phone, only to not an get answer. I was so worried I started calling hospitals and jails, only to find out he wasn't at either. I didn't get no sleep, so the next morning I was exhausted. I was on probation for my attendance at school and had one more day to miss before I was dropped. Welp, that was the last day.

Cheleste called me early that morning, crying and venting to me. As always her and Wheezy was into it. He came home at 9:00AM. She got up to release her bladder from the huge baby boy she was carrying, and found a receipt floating in the toilet. She picked the tweezers up off the countertop and pulled the wet paper out. She squinted to confirm she was seeing right with the ink wearing away. It was for the purchase of a box of condoms and his favorite drink, Hennessy. After she found that she quickly went to his pockets to inspect. Her heart stopped when she found another receipt that was from the Red Room Inn and Suites. With it few weeks before her due date her main concern was getting the baby here safe because most of her pregnancy she was stressed out. She didn't say nothing to him, she packed her an overnight bag and left. Not long after we hung up the phone Cheleste was knocking on my door with puffy eyes from crying. Both of us upset, we decided to put together the few dollars we had and got us a room. I took some weed from the smoke stash, and we were out. Nobody knew where we were and we wanted it to be that way.

After we checked in, we both jumped on each bed. We laid there, vented, cried and chilled. Me and Cheleste had more of an understanding of each other. We grew up raising ourselves. Unlike Stephanie, we were not spoon fed. Cheleste's life was not as hard as mine, but it was not easy either.

Warning Before Destruction

The next morning we woke up, got breakfast, showered and checked out the room. Back to hell holes we went. I was still in the process of forgiving Cheryl for putting me out a day after my graduation and not supporting me. I felt like if she took me then she should have done what a real mother would do and support no matter what. She always says she gives tough love, but I call it not giving a fuck. Me and Steven were also working on our bond as daughter and father. It was a lot of patching up to do from all the time he was gone. I had a heart full of anger, that was one of the main reasons I could not keep my hands to myself. Fighting seemed like it let off steam.

When I got home, Antwan was sitting on the couch playing his game. He called a few times last night, but I did not feel the need to answer. He paused the game and looked at me, asking, "So, you just going to leave and not answer the phone?" This was my first time ever doing it and I can tell he was pissed. My saying was always *I don't get mad, I get even.*

"I thought it was okay to do so," I replied slickly. I always had a slick tongue; it was the Scorpio in me.

"Now you want to start with the smart remarks, Rochelle. You know I be high and not out here doing shit.

I was at Shawn house passed out." He started reaching for his phone.

"Well you need to find a new choice of drug, because I don't think I can put up with it too much longer. I told you in the beginning one thing I will not tolerate is you not coming home at night." He cocked his head to the side as if he had the audacity. "I come in this bitch every night and you should too!" I yelled as a tear fell down my face. One thing Antwan hated was to see me cry, especially if he was the reason. I told him all I went through growing up.

He threw the controller, hopped up and started hugging me. "Come here. Listen, dry that shit. I already told you, I'm not checking for these hoes out here. You are the only now and forever, lil' woman." As I cried on his shoulder, he started to tell me how sorry he was, and it would not happen again. As my sobs began to slow down, he started kissing on my neck and moving his hands down my pants. He knew my weakness and my hot spot.

He placed his fingers in my waiting pussy as my juices began to flow gently from his touch. It was something about make up sex that drove me wild, and he knew that. He picked me up and carried me to the bed, laying me down and giving me the best orgasm my body had ever experienced. My pussy belonged to him and he knew this. He flipped me over to doggy style my ass.

"Mm, baby, deeper." I pleaded. My man's dick was memorizing. He knew how to stoke every angle. I tossed this pussy back on him as he began to pound me harder and harder.

"Damn, this some good pussy! Ahhhh! Fuck! Girl!" He pulled out, cuming all over my amped ass, later rubbing it in.

We took a shower together and went out to eat. Once again, this nigga had me back wrapped up and back falling for him and his bullshit. It never really crossed my mind that Antwan was cheating on me. Hell, my insecure ass was always in his phone, so if he was fucking around, he was doing a damn good job at it. He was gone a lot of the time, but when dealing with a street nigga you must understand, if you do not want a broke nigga then you must deal with a busy nigga.

Cheryl had a good job at a place called Defender which was an authorized dealer for ADT security. I knew it would not be long before I was ready to leave Antwan, so I felt like I needed to get me a job so I could stay afloat. Cheryl put in an application for me online which I had no idea about. She must have known shit was getting rocky my way. One thing she always made sure she instilled in me was to always make sure you hustle for your own money and never give someone the access to tell you and yours when and where you can eat. Since I was younger, Cheryl would always call her friends and Mama Latifah to tell them the most recent talk about little ol' me, Rochelle Brown, so I always made it my focus to tell her as least as possible. People knowing things about me really bothered me. I was always worried about what a person would say. I really did not want to get a weak ass 9 to 5 but I needed to make sure I was straight. Going back home to Cheryl's house was not an option for me. I still had it set in my head even though I fucked up in school I could still prove her wrong and make things happen to be successful here in Indianapolis.

I got a strange call from a number that I was unfamiliar with. "Hello. My name is Adam from Defender Direct, an authorized dealer for ADT security, and I am calling for Rochelle Brown."

I was so confused on how I applied for a job and didn't know. "This is her speaking." I replied with my proper voice in full effect.

"Yes, I received your application and would like to set up an interview with you here in the office. Is that okay?" He asked.

Still confused I asked him, "What company are you with? And what position are you hiring for?"

"We sell and monitor security systems for ADT Security. This is a customer service job. Is it something you are still interested in?" he asked me.

"Sure, what day and time would you like to meet?" I asked. *Fuck it, I will go see what this is all about.* He set up the interview within the next few days of calling. This was a real job, making good money. I was nervous to have an interview.

Antwan not coming home became something of the normal for him. Regardless of it becoming a habit for him I, each time, would still be worried about him. On top of his drug use he was diagnosed with a sleeping disorder and ADHD which he took pills for as well. After a few more times of coming in begging me to stay, telling me how sorry he was and then having good make up sex, I was fed the fuck up. I had a good feeling I was going to get the job, so I had to hold out if I could with the fights and arguments. What you call it? Picking your battles? Like Sandal would do, I quietly planned, so when I moved out, I would not be in such a fucked-up situation.

For the first time since we got together, I had to deal with anther bitch calling my phone, telling me about my nigga. That is the most embarrassing shit to me. Do not let nobody come to you and tell you shit about your mate. It was a bitch who hated me in high school. I have always been an overthinker, and if you don't tell me what is going on, then I am going to put shit together and assume that's what happened. The stories I made up in my head were always for the worst. My life has had so much bad shit going on, I got used to the bad shit. I started to feel like my life was cursed.

I got a phone call from the bitch named Ashley. She was in her feelings and felt like she needed to let me know what was going on with her and Antwan. I was hurt because I never expected him to be cheating on me.

I received a call from Defender Direct again. With a face full of tears I got myself together. It was Adam telling me he liked me, and he would like to offer me the position. It was for good pay. Hell, $12.50 an hour was good for me to not have a degree. As bad I did not want to work a 9 to 5 job, I accepted the offer. I called Cheryl to tell her about my job.

"What's up, Rochelle?" She answered the phone.

With excitement in my voice I told her, "I got a great paying job here at Defender Direct!"

"Good to hear that. I put in an application for you a few weeks ago. This is a great job with benefits, so you need to be serious about taking this position. How is everything else going?"

"I was wondering how they got my information. Thank you so much and I am going to do the right thing. Everything else is going good for me." I lied like always because I did not want to hear, "I told you so!" from her. I knew she was just waiting for that time to come.

"You still haven't gotten your money from Social Security?"

I knew that question was coming, and like I have been telling her lies, I just continued to. "No, I think the address change slowed up the process." I had no intentions of telling her the truth and didn't see a reason to. It was my money.

Stephanie and Cheleste always fucked with me asking, "Why are you so worried about what Cheryl has to say and how she feels? The way that she treats you, she doesn't give two fucks about you, girl." They were always on my ass about shit that I was oblivious to. Some areas I was handicap in and had to lean on Cheryl for her help. Shit like filling out my tax forms for my first job.

After the phone call with Cheryl I was more hurt and angrier. Tears began to flow again as I sat and waited for him to come home. My mind was idling. They say an idling mind is the devil's playground. Shortly after gathering my thoughts Antwan walked in the house. He had no idea he was walking into a ball of fire. I was pissed at this point, ready to knock his head off his shoulders at the sight of his face.

He came in like shit was cool, but I immediately lost my cool, screaming to the top of my lungs with tears rolling down my eyes, "I FUCKING HATE YOU, CHEATING ASS BASTARD! Four years I held you down through all our bullshit and this is how you pay me back?" I leaped over the couch that was by the front door and started swinging on him.

He had no idea what I was saying because I was yelling so loud. He put his arms up to protect himself from my hits. He finally got fed up and bear-hugged me, picking me up and carrying me to the room. He tossed me on the bed and put all his weight on me as I continued to scream, cry and break loose from the hold he had on me. I finally calmed down for a second and he released me from his hold. Now that I was talking calmly, he knew what the issue was. Of course he denied everything, but all the shit she was telling me was adding up to him being with her. Like always when shit got real, he called Marsha. He was such a mama's boy, it started to piss me off. After shit calmed down, it was back escalated.

Warning Before Destruction

He threw a boot at me hitting me in my head as I was packing my shit and called me a "stupid bitch." I lost it at that point. I picked up a drawer from the dresser and flung it across the room at him, he ducked, and it missed him. Still exchanging words at the top of our lungs I picked up another drawer and tossed it across the room, he dodged that one as well. There was an iron sitting on the edge of the dresser. I was sure this time I would not miss. I launched the iron at him, busting his forehead. Blood started to leak from his head instantly. Still full of rage I was still ready to hurt him. His phone was sitting on the floor. As I tried to pick it up, he grabbed the other end. I pulled the phone with all my strength as it broke into two pieces. Somehow, we fought all the way to the front room. He finally got me out of the house. I was tired of fighting, and at this point I was ready to go. I sat Indian style on the concrete in front of the apartment as I continued to holler and yell slick things.

He started throwing all my clothes out the front door on the doorstep. "YOU REALLY FUCKED UP IN THE HEAD! YOU GOT TO GO, BITCH!" He yelled as I was outside putting my clothes in the large black trash bags.

Every time we would have an argument, the first thing he would yell is I don't have shit, and I can get out of his house and give him his car back. From that point forward, I had my mind made up, I would never give another human the power to tell me when, what and how I can eat.

Up walked Marsha. She was yelling, "What the hell is going on?"

I had a lot of respect for his mother because she took me in as her own and helped me in a lot of ways without asking for anything in return. But at this point I was angry and ready to go to war with any and everybody. Stephanie was not home which was a good thing because that probably would have been the day me and her had to fight against each other and not with each other. "Your son is a liar and a cheater. I am fucking..." Before I could finish my sentence, he came with another handful of my clothes yelling.

"Antwan what happened?" she yelled as she gasped for air after seeing the blood leaking down his face. "O no, you have to go, Rochelle," she said as I continued to put my clothes in bags.

"I am not going nowhere until I have all my shit out this house!" I told her.

"Well, if you put your hands on him again while I am here, I will call the police and have you locked up. You have lost your mind!" She yelled as she stood in the doorway while Antwan continued to throw my shit out.

All I moved in with was my clothes and that was all I wanted to take with me. Marsha picked up her phone while still standing in the doorway and called Cheryl to let her know what was going on. That was the last thing I wanted to happen, for Cheryl to know I had been acting a fool again.

"I am just calling to let you know Rochelle is over here acting crazy. She busted Antwan's face by throwing an iron at him. I am telling you now if she hits him again, I am calling the police on her and I will have her locked up. She has lost her mind, and she cannot come back here so I have no clue where she is even going once she has all her shit."

"Well, thanks for the call. Please tell her to come to my house as soon as she is done getting her things packed up." Cheryl replied.

Once I got all my shit packed into the Concorde, I sat in the parking lot balling my eyes out. I was experiencing so many emotions, thinking I was right for busting his shit because he was cheating on me, but also thinking I was wrong and took shit too far. My anger, like always, got the best of me and landed me in a fucked-up position.

My thoughts were to play everything cool until I was able to stack a few checks and move, but things did not go as planned. I made sure I grabbed me some smoke from his smoke sack for the last time. I did not have a dollar to my name and nowhere to go. I stopped at the gas station and got me a pack of swishers to roll up and smoke while I figured out what my next plan was. Calling Cheryl was the last thing I wanted to do and hearing her mouth while I am still upset would just stem to me and her getting into an argument, or even a fight because I had so much anger still built up inside of me.

Chapter 9

Homeless

Cheleste and Wheezy were the only people I could ask to stay with for a while until I got a few checks, but they were living in Wheezy's father's house with enough people, and she was focused on having her baby. Antwan and his family were my family and all I have really been knowing since I was out on my own. I never had blood family and it was something that bothered me a lot. I could not understand how I had a mom and dad but no family. I felt like I was falling in the same tracks as Sandal with the moving constantly. After a few hours of riding around I finally decided to make that call.

"Mom." I paused for a minute as tears began to roll down my eyes.

The pause was so long Cheryl began calling my name to make sure I was still on the phone. "Rochelle! Rochelle, are you still there?" She called me.

"Yes! I am still here. I am homeless and need a place to stay. Can I come stay with you for a few weeks until I get my first few checks?" I asked her as bad as I did not want to. She told me yes, but also gave me a long speech. I just sat and listened. At this point I was exhausted mentally and physically and just wanted to pass out so I could wake up the next day with a clear mind to make this shit make sense. I went to her house and passed out.

Patricia was on her way back home from Fort Valley College. She became too unfocused and had collected up a few enemies as well while she was away. After all the freedom and fun she just experienced on her own in college she was not planning on staying with Mama Latifah and Babe Musa too long. The next day I called Patricia and we talked for hours, getting caught up on all the shit we've been through the past 2 years. We agreed we would get an apartment together and be roommates. From the living situation with Antwan and Stephanie I told myself I would never be roommates with anyone again, but at this point I had to do what was best for me. Our apartment hunt began immediately.

It was finally my first day of work. All I could think about was getting these few checks and moving into my place. I liked the job. Cheryl worked in the financial department of the company, so her desk was upstairs. We started working back on our relationship. While I knew I needed to forgive and forget it was a hard pill to swallow to forget the bullshit Cheryl pulled.

Patricia began job hunting. Within 3 weeks we had us a nice 2-bedroom, 2 full bathroom apartment on the westside of Indianapolis. Cheryl was back living with her parents, so she gave me her queen size bed, plus a dresser, nightstand, and tall drawer. Now was the time to get my life back on track and not let another nigga come in and fuck things up for me. I was doing good on my job and had plans to enroll back in college. My hustle and motivation to be better was strong, but it seemed like no matter how much I tried to stay focused I was always knocked back down by some bullshit. I only knew the basic things to living because of Cheryl. Other than that, nobody taught me shit. I had to raise myself and figure everything out on my own.

Me and Patricia were too young to get in the over 21 club, so we had fake ID's made. We planned our first night out. We got cute in our heels and headed to the newest, hottest club in the city which was only 10 minutes from me and Patricia's place. This club had a dress code— no flats for the ladies, no hats for men, no tennis shoes, and no sagging allowed. We were only 19 and 20 but we were on our grown woman shit. Every weekend going out became our thing. We went out so much the security guard started letting us walk right in.

We lived close to a westside hood called 2G. Patricia knew a nigga named Donald who lived in 2G. We went to meet up with him at the hood candy store for a second.

Patricia got out and switched across the street as I sat in the car. A few minutes of sitting there, a 2005 Suzuki Grand Vitara pulled up next to me. I always paid close attention to my surroundings because I needed to be the first to see anything suspicious, especially being in this rough ass hood.

The driver pulled up, hit his blunt a few times and hopped out. As I was breaking my neck to stare, out hopped a fine ass black man with dreads down the middle of his back. He had on a leather coat with some fresh ass Nikes, a button up, and some pants so creased and fresh from the dry cleaners they barely moved. He had all kinds of chains hanging from his neck, rings on almost every finger and some diamond earrings that were blinging in the sunlight. He had a knot of money in his pocket sticking out. Everything about him said money. My window was cracked so when he hopped out, I got a nose full of the fresh ass weed he was smoking. We made eye contact and he gave a head nod like *what's up*. I smiled, showing my perfect white teeth that Cheryl had paid good money for and gave him a nod back. I was talking on the phone to Cheleste, and in the middle of our conversation I drifted off and heard nothing she was saying. His dreads swung as he got out of the SUV and walked across the street to the candy store.

"Bitchhhhhhh, I just seen the finest man on earth, and he looks and smells like big money." I told her.

Cheleste was the hype man, so her being herself she egged me on to get his number. Patricia came back out a few minutes after he walked in.

I had to see if she knew who he was since he was in Donald's hood. "Girl! Who was the fine piece of chocolate that just walked into the store?" I asked before she was even all the way in the car.

"That is Bryce, but the hood calls him DBoy. He is one of the biggest street niggas out here with money. He is that nigga out here pushing big weight. He knows Donald." She told me.

Damn, all that sounded good to me. I was addicted to street niggas, and I was not leaving that candy store until got his phone number. "Hold on bitch, do not pull off yet. I need him in my life!" I said, forgetting Cheleste was even on the phone.

Seconds later he came walking out of the candy store with his long, freshly twisted dreads swaying side to side. As he walked to his truck door, we locked eyes again. He came to my window as I rolled it down. I was looking a mess from still moving and getting things set up. "How you are doing?" he asked with a handful of Swishers.

"I am good, sexy. Excuse how I look, I am in the process of moving into my spot."

"You all good. You smoke? Drink?" he asked me with a sexy grin.

"I drink a little, but I do smoke." I replied blushing.

"Give me your number and we can link up later and have a session," he replied while pulling both phones out his pocket. We exchanged numbers, he got in his car and pulled off, so did we.

I was geeked and looking forward to his call later that night. Me and Patricia cleaned up our house, smoked, listened to some music and had a few wine coolers to drink. Donald had a sting who sold us a nice furniture set and some living room tables. Our shit was coming along well.

About 9:00PM that night my phone rang from an unfamiliar number. I figured it was DBoy calling so I put my sexy voice on and answered. "Hello?"

"What's up, little mama?" he asked.

"Chilling at home, playing cards with my aunt and having a drink. What's up with you?" I replied, blushing all over again.

"Damn, can I come chill with you and put a few in the air?"

Warning Before Destruction

From the smoke that seeped out of his car earlier he had some good shit. Me and Patricia was balling on a budget so we had smoke but it was some "Reggie" which happened to be the most brown, dirty weed with seeds in it, the shit that was $5 a gram. "Yeah, that's cool, I'll send you my address, and the gate code to get in is pound four, one, five, zero."

I was nervous, I had butterflies in my stomach. I sent him the address and continued me and Patricia's girl's night in the peace and quiet of our own home. A few hours later my phone rang again, and it was DBoy telling me he was outside. I told him the door to come to. I met him at the door still with butterflies in my stomach. He greeted me with a hug. Donald came over that night too, so him and Patricia were laid up.

He walked in and we went straight to my room. He pulled out his smoke, looked at me and said, "Can you roll up?"

I giggled because I was a professional at rolling now. I replied, "Yeah, I can pearl a blunt."

He laughed and handed me the weed and Swisher. Like the fuck I told Patricia, he had some good smoke that was called Doughty. The smell came out the top of the jar as he opened it. When I broke it down to roll it up, it was sticky with no seeds and no sticks. It was that $10-gram shit.

We sat, smoked, talked and listened to music. We exchanged information about each other. Come to find out he was 31 and he said he had 6 kids but claimed a lot of other kids as well. He told me he had a vasectomy and could not have anymore kids. He swore he did not have a woman, but I was not stupid. I knew with all the money, the flashy clothes, cars and shoes also came with a gang of hoes. He asked me was that too old being I was only 19. Nope, he was not too old for me.

After we smoked and talked, we both laid in the bed and cuddled. His phone was vibrating all damn night on the nightstand. I knew he had 2 phones, but I also knew he sold drugs.

As I laid on my side and he was behind me, holding me, we both woke up. He started kissing on my neck from behind and lightly grinding his dick against my ass. I reached my hand back and started rubbing and caressing his dick as it slowly grew harder and harder in my hand. Next thing I knew he was pulling my panties off and teasing my pussy to make it wet. He slowly slid his huge black dick inside of me, pulling me closer and closer as I slowly ran across the bed, away from the dick. He kept pulling me closer and closer, giving me hard strokes. He slowly pulled his dick out and slowly slid it back in, once again teasing my little wet, tight pussy. He pulled out again and climbed on top me of. While sucking my titties he slowly went inside of me, going balls deep.

After 10 more minutes of great dick, he came all over my stomach and chest, even shooting some on my lip. The freak in me needed a taste of this man. Yep, I licked it off. He moaned even more like that was a big turn on for him. I got up and went to get hot, wet towels for him to wipe himself off, went back to rinse the towel out and made it nice and warm for him again.

He whispered, "Just let the towel sit on my dick."

I did as he asked and went back in my bathroom to wipe myself off. His phone was still going off, but he didn't pay it no mind, and neither did I. After our nice session of sex followed by a blunt, it was time for him to get back to the money as he said. That phone ringing the way it was seemed a little suspicious to me, but who was I to ask this man about his phone ringing when he was not my man?

He gave me a hug, grabbed my ass and said, "I will call you in a minute."

As I blushed and shut the door behind him, I replied, "Okay, baby."

As soon as he left, Patricia came running to my room so we could get caught up on each other's night. Patricia made us breakfast as we sat and talked in the kitchen.

Chapter 10
Addicted to A Dope Boy

Antwan finally reached out to me. He was telling me how much he missed us. After the good dick I just got from this fine ass older man, Antwan was no longer a thought in my mind. I did miss him, but grudges were a big thing, I had a hard time letting go. I held a grudge once again for putting me out on the streets with nowhere to go. I had to explain to him that the shit between me and him was dead. After the conversation he told me since I was done with him that I needed to bring him his car. I begged and pleaded for him to allow me more time in his car so I could get around, as well as back and forth to work.

He started yelling, "No, you got a new nigga, Tee!"

I hung up, only to shortly receive a call from Marsha. I had the upmost respect for her, but at this point I was pissed she would allow her son to come take the car from me. Me and Marsha had some words with each other which made her cry. Marsha called Stephanie and Antwan to let them know the hurtful things I said to her. First Stephanie called. We had a yelling match and that was the end of that. Seconds later Antwan called cussing me out as well. I told him I will leave his car in the Wendy's parking lot with the key under the seat and he can get it from there. I knew I lost a friendship with Stephanie.

Me and Cheryl were seeing each other daily from working at the same place. We were still working on creating a bond, but I still felt like some of my business was not hers. Telling her I was messing with a man who was 11 years older than me was something I had no plans on telling her. Hearing her mouth was something I tried to prevent whenever I could, because she always had a mouth full to say, especially when it was something wrong.

Me and DBoy became tight and started hanging out with each other often. He was a well-known, respected, hustling gangster with pockets and safes full of money, as well as many women, kids and baby mamas. The hood and street nigga in him turned me on. DBoy had a main bitch who was also the mother of his kids. Her name was Shae. She had his youngest child as well as his only girl. That is where all his stuff was at as far as clothes, shoes and cars. He had good money. Hell, he been selling drugs all his life, even caught his first body at the age of 15. Money was his focus, he loved the finer things in life. Looking for a legal way of income he just brought a house right outside of his hood. He was in the process of gutting the house out and redoing the inside.

I started hanging with him and making runs. He sold hard, soft and even wet sticks which is cigarettes with embalming fluid on it. That shit was so strong I could smell it as soon as he opened the bottle. Whenever he needed anything fixed, he would call one of his "stings" and they would come running and get whatever it was he needed done for him. Having a young pretty thing on his side, his niggas would always tell him how cute I was, and he would reply the same all the time: "Man, you ain't had fun until you had something young." Our sex life was wild, and I made sure each time to give him the best because I knew he had bitches and I needed to make sure that I stayed number one on the list.

I told him about my car and my ex. He told me not to worry about it and he would help me get around. As time went on, he would give me money, was paying my bills and I always got whatever it was that I requested. He started to leave his stuff here and there at my house from his drugs to clothes. We were on a schedule. He would spend the night, drop me off at work, pick me up, take me home to clean, leave for a minute and come back. He had me cooking like I was his wife or some shit. He was obsessed with fishing. Many days a week he would go fishing, bring the full fish home, cut the head off and clean it, leaving me to cook it.

Shae was a worrisome ass bitch. None of his baby mamas called as much as she did. She would call for him to babysit because her nose was running, just something so little and dumb. I think she knew at this point he was spending time with someone new. One morning after a nice session and cuddles, here goes the damn phone blowing up like it did the first night.

"If I did not answer then it's evident I am busy, Shae. What do you need?" He answered the phone with much irritation in his voice.

"I have surgery tomorrow for my carpal tunnel, and I need you to be here to help me with the kids." She spoke quietly.

"We already had this conversation; I will be there later." Becoming more and more frustrated with her calling all the damn time, he nearly tossed his phone onto the floor.

When I knew he was with her or any of his other bitches I would always play my role and keep calm. I would not nag, fuss or cuss. I knew when it was my time, it was my time, and I didn't want to fuck up what we had going on. When he was away, I would never blow his phone up. I knew my role and I played it well. I knew he was fucking with me because I was not one to brag or blow his phone up, plus, I did not have any kids. I eventually met his kids, but he kept Shae's kids away from the thought of them telling her.

Spending the night at my apartment became the norm. I would often vent to him about Patricia and her nasty ways. She was something like a hoarder like her mom and dad was. It was an argument we had often, especially the kitchen area. Laying in the bed, me and DBoy heard a BOOM, BOOM and yelling. It seemed close to our doorway. I got up out the bed, put on my robe and went to see what the problem was. The front door to the apartment was opened, and all kinds of clothes, furniture, and shoes were piled up in the hallway coming into my room. There was Patricia and DJ arguing. It had been a week since she had spoken to him. The night before she was telling me DJ said he was going out of town for a job. Well, within that week she spoke to him once. She found out he was with his other girlfriend and Patricia told him to come get his shit, she was done, but instead of being an adult he decided to come and tear our house up, moving all the furniture we purchased from his sting out the living room, some of the shit in her room and all his clothes and shoes. I was pissed, and with my shitty attitude and ruthless mouth I let her have it. No way in the hell she should have let that little weak ass nigga come in here and take shit. After this I was fed up and so was DBoy.

"You don't need a roommate no more, you got me" He said, fed up after we were woke up from her mess.

"So, what you are saying, baby?" I asked shyly as I laid on his chest.

"It's time to look for a new place. Well, with me and you. I will help you on all the bills. This ain't for us." He was talking to me as if I were a child.

I reminded him I will be moving out with absolutely nothing. But he had all the money, he paid the cost to be the boss, so I was very submissive to him. I knew if something got fucked up, he was the man and could get it fixed, or he'll just buy a new one. Everyone was telling me messing with older men, they mold you to be what they want you to be. He taught me so much in the last four months of us fucking around, from the streets, to common sense, to how to be on my grown woman shit.

I knew telling Patricia I was moving out was going to cause a big problem between us. However, I had to listen to my man. I waited a few days after me and DBoy had the conversation to bring it to Patricia. Even though she was working, I did not know if she could handle all the bills by herself. As for me I had my nigga, so I knew I was cool.

While on my lunch break, I decided to call her. "Wassup, girl? You busy?" I whispered while in the breakroom.

"Nah, what's up?" At this point we barely been talking since all the bullshit happened with her and DJ, so she probably knew this was coming.

"Well, I am about to move into a one-bedroom apartment. I already spoke to the leasing agency. You can sign the lease over to me completely or we can terminate the lease and it will go against both of us." I told her, letting her know of the choices she had.

"Ugh, I knew this was coming. Well, give me a few days and I will let you know what I decide to do, Rochelle. You are putting me in a very fucked up situation." She said very upset.

"Okay, well, next month's rent is due in a few days, so we need to know as soon as possible." I was still being as nice as I could be.

The fucking nerve of you to rush—"

I hung up before things got heated between us to avoid me being rude. I just decided to let shit work themselves out.

Antwan called me out the blue whining and crying about missing me, but I was too wrapped up in DBoy to even fall for his shit.

I just sat and listened to all the shit he had to say. My reply was "you knew what you had, you just thought you could never lose me." And hung up the phone.

Even though DBoy had many bitches and his main bitch I still did not want to entertain nobody else, and the way DBoy was set up, he was not going for me fucking around with nobody else. I got Antwan's name tatooed on my titty back when me and him were together and DBoy hated it, every chance he got to talk shit about it he did.

One day he gave me the money, told me to go get that shit covered up, and my submissive ass did just that. The next day I had an appointment to get the tattoo covered up. I was obsessed with ink anyway, so I got a flower to cover it up.

Sandal's brother still had the trust fund for me since I did not go to school and I was still in need of a car. At this point the whole family was upset with me for not going away to college and even more upset that I did not finish college at the community college. I was nervous to call and ask but I had to suck up my pride and make that phone call. After hearing my uncle's mouth about how upset he was he finally agreed to send me the money.

It was a major drug bust in 2G. As me and DBoy laid in the bed and watched the news he was up getting his clothes on to go get his shit from the trap house. He went to get all his guns, 7 pounds of weed, 127 grams of crack, and his embalming fluid or wet as we called it and brought it all back to my apartment. That was another main reason he wanted us to have our own place because him stashing shit at my place was becoming the norm. After loading my house up with his shit, he told me that he needed to talk to me. As always, we smoked a fat blunt while talking.

"You know what is going on here. I have to go to Florida for a while until shit clears up here. You know our business is our business, so nobody needs to know what is going on or what I have here. I am trusting you and hope you don't fuck it up."

"I don't know shit is the answer and will always be just that when it comes to these people. I am just a little sad that you are leaving me for such a long time," I replied as I passed the blunt back to him.

"I know, baby, but this is something that has to be done. You got a smoke sack here, I will leave you some cash flow and you will be straight. Daddy coming back home to you." He always called himself daddy. He fucked me good and cut out.

Chapter 11
Nothing like my Own

Patricia went to the leasing office and finally decided she would sign the lease over to me. I was able to downsize to a one-bedroom apartment. I did not make any moves without checking with DBoy first so I called him to let him know we got approved to move to a one bedroom. He told me to let them know I will be moving within the next few weeks. Everything was going good. I had a nigga who loved me and gave me the world. I was about to move into my own place, still working my punk ass 9 to 5 and my uncle finally sent me the money, so as soon as DBoy got back he was going to the auction for me.

While DBoy was gone out of town I started getting a lot of private calls. The person was not saying nothing, just sitting on the phone until I hung up. While DBoy was gone, many of my calls went unanswered, which normally happened when he was with Shae.

The last private call the caller finally decided to speak on this call. "Hello, umm, yeah, I seen this number in my man's phone and I was just seeing what is going on?" This bitch was curious.

"Well, who is your man and who are you?" I replied. I figured I will start this convo off nice before my smart-ass remarks came. I already knew who it was from hearing the bitch voice when she calls DBoy's phone.

"DBoy or Bryce. This number is in his phone so much I decided to call it myself." She responded quickly.

"Okay, well, just know that your man is my man as well. That's all the explanation I got for you, and stop calling my muthfucking phone." The phone hung up. I already knew it was Shae.

She texted my phone, "Let the games begin."

I replied, "I'm not worried," with the signature on my app saying *DBoy's Girl*. I was not worried about her because if I played my position in DBoy's life I knew I had a secured spot. He always tells me if you get pregnant, I am going back home, meaning back to Shae. Me and my place were his peace and I wanted to keep it that way.

DBoy was finally back home, and I missed my nigga. I found out he was with Shae from word around his hood, but I was okay with that. I figured that anyway from the calls and texts. Shae told him I was calling her phone private, so he made sure he checked me for that, but I told him as well as proved my point it was her calling my phone first. We finally got out of the two bedroom and settled into the one bedroom. Even though DeBoy did not come home to me every night I was cool with that. I knew he still had Shae who he would tell me she is just a business partner if anything, but I was far from a dummy. I knew what the fuck was going on but still playing my position to get what it was I wanted which was his time, good sex, good weed, and any material.

I still had my bedroom set but that was all I had. The next day after we moved in, he gave me $1,500 and told me to go get everything I needed for the apartment as well as furniture for my living room and dining room. I did as I was told, and my first home was finally comfy and complete. He also got me a Saturn from the auction which was nothing I wanted but I had to settle at this time to have a car. DBoy had an old school money green drop top. Of course, I rode passenger often as we rode out to make his money runs. His dad was a yorkie breeder, so I also got my first animal— a Yorkie named Tyson. Everything I asked for, I got it. No questions asked from him.

Patricia moved back home with her parents. Our relationship started to get shaky because of the way DBoy would do me. Patricia, Cheleste and Stephanie would always remind me how dumb I was for him, but I did not care. That was my nigga regardless if he came home one night a week. Cheleste was still in a fucked-up situation with Wheezy, Patricia was a big hoe, and Stephanie was desperate for love so it was nothing them bitches could say to me to leave my nigga alone. I lived out west and they lived out east. We were all busy still trying to get a hold of this thing called life, so we did not talk often.

As me and DBoy got closer and closer I began to learn more and more things about him. He started to get more comfortable around me, introducing me to things. He always rode around with a gun on his hip, and always instilled in me that if we ever encountered the police tell them the gun was mine. He was a serious violent felon so he would serve time off top. Being his down ass bitch, I knew the game plan and if we were ever under pressure, folding was something I refused to do. He was a real-life thug. He had a few pit bulls which he kept at Shae's house. It was in his daily routine to go condition his dogs, make them run the treadmill for hours at a time, fed them a certain way, and made sure he walked them. The dogs were so big he had to walk them on huge chains. I never knew the reason he cared for those dogs so much until one day he invited me to a dog fight. It was good money for him to bet on these fights.

Warning Before Destruction

Before we walked in as always when we were doing illegal shit, he gave me the pep talk. You don't know nothing. I was a very shy and quiet girl. I always sat back and kept it classy, stayed in my lane. DBoy would always express he loved that about me and that's why he did not mind taking me places with him. We walked into the house through a side door and down to a basement where it was a big open area but fenced off space for the dog fight to happen. It was the nastiest thing I've ever seen. The dogs just fought and fought until one finally died. Blood and spit were being thrown all over. DBoy's dog won, all bruised, scratched and limping he just got $5,000. He got his money and the dog as we left. The other dog laid there dead. Not asking any questions as I was taught by DBoy I didn't say shit.

Cooking his crack in my apartment was something else he became very comfortable with doing. I watched so much before I knew it, I was in the kitchen for his ass whipping up shit whenever he was not able to. I also became his runner. When he was not available, I would make the runs for him, serving whatever it was that was needed. I never seen so much money in my life. The nights DBoy did come home to me, the first thing he did was throw all his money on the bed and make me count it, as well as put it together nice and neatly.

Warning Before Destruction

The house DBoy started remodeling was coming together well. His stings always got him right. Robbing people was another form of getting money for him. Being that I worked at a security system place he would often ask me questions to get in business accounts. I always looked in systems for different companies but because we were just a dealer for ADT, we did not have that information in our systems. Many late nights he would leave out in all black, but once again like I was told, didn't ask no questions.

Yearly my job would have family day weekends at an amusement park. This year was at Kentucky Kingdom which was about 1 hour and 30 minutes south of where we lived. I asked DBoy if he wanted to go and without a doubt, he said yes.

The following week we were packed up and ready to go. I was excited for some one on one time with my man away from everybody else. He got us a rental and we left. The ride was sweet. We just rode, listened to music, talked and smoked. I became the fulltime blunt roller when it was time to smoke, having blunt after blunt rolled up and ready for him at his request. We pulled up to the nice ass hotel room which I had previously booked, we checked into our room, dropped our bags off and went out to eat. It was not long before Shae started blowing his phone up, and like always when he answered she did not want shit. We went back to the room, showered together, smoked a few blunts, had a great sex session and passed out.

The next day I was waking up out of my sleep by DBoy saying, "Baby, let's get up, go eat and go shopping."

I woke right up, showered and ironed our clothes for the day. While I was ironing, I overheard DBoy talking on the phone to one of his bitches in the bathroom, basically saying he was out of town on a business trip and he would make it up to her when he got back. I was in my feelings about it, but I knew if I questioned him, he would snap, plus like always I knew my position and at this time I was getting all his time and energy. After we ate good, we went to the mall. He told me to get whatever it was that I wanted. I never had designer shit, so I just stuck with what I knew. Victoria Secret was the first place on my list. I went in there and spent $50.00 on panties. Since Cheryl took me in she always shopped for me at Learner's or New York and Company, so that was the next spot on my list. There I spent about $130.00 on clothes. At Claire's Accessories I spent $40.00 on accessories. He made it all about me. Man, I felt like a queen walking out with all those bags.

Warning Before Destruction

We had tickets to Kentucky Kingdom Amusement Park from my job. That was the next place on our list. We had a good time like we were 2 big kids. He won me a few teddy bears from playing games, we got to see all kinds of cartoon characters, and we rode damn near every ride in the park. It was a really nice time. At home when we spent time together it was ripping and running the streets, hitting stings, so to be away, just me and him out having fun, I soaked it all up. I took many pictures of him and us, but I was never allowed to post them on my Facebook page due to the many bitches he had, as well as him being so known in Indianapolis, he did not want people to know nothing about him.

After a fun-filled day at the amusement park we went back to the hotel, got fresh and hit the streets. He had a younger cousin who lived there with his old lady, so we went to chill with them. It was a nice time chilling, smoking, drinking, music playing and good conversation. They were telling a story about a time they were younger, a white man who owed DBoy some money was playing about giving him his shit. DBoy was crazy all his life, mind you he caught his first body at the age of 15. DBoy and his cousin kidnapped the man, tied him up in the back of his car, and made him smoke 4 wet sticks. The man was so high he shit and pissed on himself, so they put him in the trunk of the car. They drove the man all the way to Kentucky. DBoy had his pit bull with him which got loose when they got there so as they went to look for the dog they were caught by the police. As they told the story they cracked so many jokes about it. It was a great time, so we planned for them to come up to Indianapolis in a few weeks to visit us. After the visit we headed back home.

A few days after we got back from our trip, DBoy was missing for a few hours. He would never go too long without calling me back, regardless if he answered for a few seconds telling me he was busy and he would call me back, but this time I did not get a response. When we first moved into our apartment DBoy got a house phone as well just in case any emergencies occurred, and he needed to call.

Sitting at home, still wondering what the fuck is going on, the house phone rung. "Hello?" I answered on the first ring.

"You have a collect call from DBoy, an inmate at the Marion County Jail. To accept, press one."

My heart dropped as I heard the operator and I pressed one immediately to accept the phone call. "What is going on, baby?" I asked, panicking but keeping my cool so he wouldn't know.

"Man, it's some bullshit. You know we can't really wrap over this phone, but I need you to handle a few things for me so I can get right up out this muthafucka. Call Tosha for me and tell her I need her on standby for the bond money and keep calling down here to see when they give me a bond, and how much. Can you do that?" He asked as if I were slow to the game.

"Yeah, I got her number saved in my phone so I will get right on that. Do you need me to do anything else?" I asked. I was going to stand on him all the way and make sure he got home fast and not slow.

Tosha was another baby mama, but she was cool with me. It was many times me and her met up so I could give her some money per DBoy's request. Him and Tosha were like teammates. She sold drugs for him as well as herself, but he was her supplier. She caught a case for him a few years ago. They were riding when the police pulled them over but DBoy had warrants so he told her to hit the gas and send them on a high-speed chase. Like all his women, she did exactly what he said. She got caught but he ran away. That was a case she had to fight for a while. One thing about DBoy, he had his bitches in check, except Shae. She was the only bitch out of line.

After hanging up with DBoy, I did as I was told and called Tosha. "Hello."

"Yeah." She always had an attitude, but it did not bother me. I never knew if it was personal or just her. I never cared. I was just doing what my man told me to do.

"Hey, this is Rochelle. DBoy is locked up. You know he is not saying much over the phone, but he told me to call you and tell you to have bond money on hand. I will keep calling and checking to see when and if he gets a bond, and I will call you to let you know." I told her.

"Bet!" she replied, and the phone hung up.

After a day of waiting he finally got a court date, but still no bond. He told me the court date and time but told me not to come because Shae was going to be there for him. Yep, again my feelings were hurt but I did not dwell on the issue too long. My focus was getting him home. At his court date the judge set a bond. He called me right after court and told me to call Tosha so she could give me the money. Sure enough a few hours later she brought me the money, and I was headed to bond him out. DBoy made sure he called me to tell me not to come pick him up from the jail, and just to go pay his bond money. Like always when it came to him, I did what I was told to do and did not ask no questions.

I did not see him as soon as he got out, of course. I had to wait my turn, and that was exactly what I did. When he finally came over, he had his affidavit from the arrest. He sat next to me and told me to read it. The affidavit said the police got a dude named Ricky who was a white boy who worked for Dboy on the house he was rebuilding. They were doing some fraudulent shit to get all the material from Menard's to build the house. Ricky snitched on DBoy and the police pulled up to 4150 North Kessler Boulevard, which is believed to be DBoy's address, looking for him but he was not there. It went on to explain how they approached the house with the search warrant and a pregnant woman opened the door.

The pregnant woman was resisting arrest, so they handcuffed her as the other officers searched the house. The affidavit also explained it was 4 kids in the house which were placed with family members. In the house the police found some of his cocaine and weed. I remembered that address that was in the affidavit, and come to find out the pregnant bitch who they had in handcuffs was Shae. I had so many mixed emotions running thru me. He did not mention shit to me about this bitch being pregnant by him.

After I read the paper, I looked at him and whispered "Sooooooo your baby mama is pregnant by you?"

After looking confused for a minute, he looked at me and said, "Yes, she is six months pregnant. Look, I know I did not tell you about it, but right now is not the time to bitch about it. The baby will be here in December." He said with much agitation in his voice.

At that point it made me realize that's why the bitch has been playing on my phone and in her feelings because they have been fucking, but the whole time he been telling me he has not touched her. He was charged with possession and dealing of both. He was a threat to society, so they placed him on the GPS system, which was an ankle bracelet and box that kept tabs on his location 24/7.

Chapter 12
A whole Baby Later

DBoy spent many nights away from what I called "our" home, and many nights not answering my calls. He started getting to the point he would say, "I'll be home tonight" and not show, nor call to let me know what was going on. It all started taking a toll on me.

"DBoy? I know we have this understanding and my part should be played accordingly, but what I will not do is sit my ass in this house praying you make it home to me."

"Don't start this shit! You knew the fucking situation beforehand. You weren't saying all this shit spending that money a niggah was tossing your way."

"You think I need this shit in my life? Huh? I have seen low before. Hell, I've slept many nights at other people's homes not knowing if I would be able to maintain! So, don't dare think I need you or your money."

He walked off with no regards to what or how I was feeling. I sort of blamed me because, ladies, a man will only do what you allow him to do. If you put up with the shit then you may as well accept it.

Warning Before Destruction

I tried to stress the point to him, following him to the bedroom to complete my thoughts. "I know what you do, and if you not coming home then you can just tell me that."

Still, not one single word from the man I thought I had my back. It was many nights I made food or plans for him to not show. Since I was not his main bitch, holidays were very lonely for me. Of course he had to be at home with Shae and their kids. I had plans for his birthday night. Many nights leading up to that night I asked to confirm he was coming to be with me. I bought us a nice jacuzzi suite and made his favorite— my homemade lasagna with hot peppers in it. Being romantic was never an issue for me. Regardless of the 11-year age difference I did not slack and stayed on my grown woman.

I set the room up nice as well as had his blunts rolled and liquor on ice for him. I had on my sexy lingerie and was ready to have some fun, only for him to not answer the phone nor did he show up. Once again, my heart was broken, or did I cause my own pain by allowing this shit to continue? I laid in that room and cried my eyes out until that address popped up in my head. Yep, it was time I did a drive by this bitch Shae's house to see if his car is outside.

Warning Before Destruction

I threw on my robe and house shoes and was out the door. I Map Quested the address and it was about 15 minutes from the hotel, and 10 minutes from my apartment. Wow, and this bitch lives close to my place. I played my music loud, lit my blunt and was on my way. It was about 12:12AM when I pulled up down the street and decided to sit and scope the scene out for a minute. Still with tears in my eyes I was making sure I didn't miss a beat. Yep, his car was sitting right in the driveway like that was where he was supposed to be. No activity went on that hour. You see, I was always told that if you go searching you will find. Sometimes it's your own damn heartache you run across. DBoy was spending his birthday with her and her kids.

Pulling off with my face glistening from the tears, I lit another blunt and headed back to the hotel room where I laid and cried some more until I went to sleep. The next day, I woke up, eyes puffy as fuck and with a major migraine. I did not call his phone one time to show him I was shitty, pissed off and hurt. I took a fresh hot shower, got dressed, packed the room up and went home.

The next day around 6:00PM, after I stayed busy all day so I would not call or text him, I finally heard his key unlocking the door. When he walked in, I refused to pay him any attention at all. I continued sitting on my couch watching TV.

"Babyyyyy!" he said with a smile as he walked in the house.

What I didn't get was why this fool came up in here laughing. I was going to make sure he knew this situation was not a joke to me. "I missed the joke, and I am lost as to why you are walking in here smiling."

"I got caught up. Do not start that bitching. I already told you in the beginning I don't come home every night!" He looked at me and said at this point with the most serious face.

"And like I told you, I understand all of that, but I asked you all night are you going to make it. Just like your time is valuable, and you hate waiting, I am the same too. You basically said fuck me." As a tear slowly rolled down my face.

"You did not even ask me what happened. You instantly snapped on me, so let's go back to the part where you ask what happened?" he said, starting to get more and more upset from all the smart ass comments I made back.

"Because you are full of shit, and I know no matter how much proof I got you are going to fucking lie!" I yelled. I went from 0 to 10 REAL QUICK. The fact that I rode past that bitch Shae house and he was there but was still lying to me made me want to reach out and put my hands on him something serious, but I knew his temper and I knew if I did that then I was liable to get my ass kicked.

"Let me tell your ass something! Girl, when it comes to my kids, I'm not putting them second to nobody and that includes you!" He replied to make me feel bad, but I did not feel bad at all for going off because I knew him and was no stranger to his game.

"Blah, blah, blah... All you had to do was fucking call me. You think I give any levels of fucks about all that?" I replied as my anger started to get more and more intense from the fact he was STILL lying to my face like I wasn't shit. I could not blow my cover and let him know I was sitting outside his baby mama house and I saw his car. That just would have been another reason to flip shit on me. He was good for that, even though I know he really knew I was a good, faithful, loyal girl to his no-good cheating, lying ass. He was good at flipping shit on me to make me feel bad or guilty of some shit.

"So, now, are you telling me I'm supposed to put you before my kids, Rochelle?" he said, switching this whole argument up.

I knew my mouth, so I quickly got my keys and went for a ride. I cannot lie, this man had full control of me and he knew that. Molding me to be his bitch is what he was doing, but I kept ignoring the red flags. I was Dickmatized, blinded by his reputation in the streets, his money and the love he gave when he was not being mean. Shit, I traded everything I was as a woman for pillow talk.

Of course, when I got back, he was gone. The next morning, he snuck in with his key, waking me up to some fire ass head and a nice hard dick. After hours of make-up sex, shit was back to normal. He knew what would make me forgive him and shut up.

The end of December came quick. It was a month I was dreading to come because it was also Shae's due date. We had sex many times unprotected, I can admit his pull-out game was strong, but I was surprised I was not pregnant yet. I wanted to have his baby so bad. I wanted to have a girl because he had 5 boys and 1 girl which happened to be by Shae. Plus, he was such a great father to his kids, but then reality would set in and I could hear him saying, "If you get pregnant, I am going back home." Home for him was Shae's house.

It was a void of not really having family that made me want a child so bad. I mean Cheryl and her extended family was all I had, but they didn't understand me, and they were so distant. I only spoke to them when I reached out or when it was a family get together. So, I really felt lonely. Even though DBoy was there, sometimes there remained a void. So, hell yeah, I was in my feelings. I understood he had to be there for his baby. The days that he was with Shae were lonely as he took time to help Shae and adjust to the new baby.

As time went on DBoy started spending less and less time with Shae. He was finally at a point where he was ready to be done with her. After a few weeks he began to bring Shae's kids to our house. One thing for sure DBoy was a great father to his kids. Even to the kids he did not have biologically from all his baby mamas. I already had his 2 boys often; I was like his personal babysitter when he had the kids. He would leave and sometimes be gone all night while I had his kids. I didn't have a problem with it though because I was so wrapped up and gullible for this nigga,my womans intuitions refused to kick in.

Shit seemed like it went from good to bad real fast for me. I was headed to visit my brother in prison when I caught a flat tire. I was blowing DBoy's phone up and of course no answer. After a while I started texting him letting him know I was stuck on the side of the highway. He never came so I had to make a call to the main person who I hated to call and ask for help, Cheryl. She came right to get me and took me back to my apartment. Later that evening, like always, DBoy decided to come to my place. I told him about my car. We hopped in his car and drove up and down the highway looking for my car. It was nowhere to be found and not in the same spot I left it. I called the city county building to see if the police took my car because it was sitting on the side of the road. They told me no. I had no idea where my Saturn had gone. So, yep, now I was back at square one with no car. Depending on people was something I just could not do but I had to, and fucking with DBoy, I always had to have a plan A, B, C and D.

New Year's Eve had finally come. DBoy was nowhere to be found, so I called Patricia and asked her what her plans were and if I could join her. She always knew where the parties were and every weekend she was out and about getting drunk and dancing on the dance floor all night. She never missed a weekend of going out. She told me she was going to a house party that was supposed to be lit and invited me. I was a nervous mess because it had been a while since I talked to DBoy and I just left the house without letting him know. I was doing it out of spite because at this point, I was fed up with all his lies and bullshit, but that was my nigga and I was not going to let him go, and I had no plans to leave him either.

Patricia came to pick me up and we were off and out in the streets having a good time. After a few hours of being at the house party my phone began to ring back to back. I did not know what to do because I knew he was going to tell me he was coming to pick me up. Me and Patricia were working on our relationship even though she hated that nigga with a passion, and I knew telling her I was leaving her to be with him was going to be an issue. I finally snuck off to the bathroom where I answered the phone.

"Where the fuck you at?" he yelled over the loud music.

"I am at a house party with Patricia." I told him waiting for his reply.

"Oh, you're out whoring with your auntie. What is the address? I am about to come pick you up," he snapped. He knew Patricia got around the town and that was the main reason he did not want me to hang with her.

It was a short pause while I looked in my phone for the address to the house party we were at.

"Hello!" He yelled again.

"I am looking though my phone to get the damn address, hold on." I snapped back, already shitty I had to leave.

"Text it to me and I will be there to get you." He said and hung up.

I went back out to the living room and sat next to Patricia to have my last drink before he pulled up. I did not want to tell her he was coming so I waited until the very last minute when he was outside to let her know where I was going. He pulled up and text me "come on". I told Patricia I was leaving with DBoy and he was already outside to pick me up. She had an attitude, she rolled her eyes at me and walked away. I knew she was mad at me, but when my man called, I had to go running. I eventually had to stop venting to Patricia about DBoy because the hate she began to have for him was so serious.

I got in the car to him asking me a thousand questions about the house party. I was still pissed at him for not coming home the night before, but I played it cool.

"Can you make some meatloaf for dinner?" I knew he was going to ask me to cook him dinner like he did on the nights he decided to be with me.

We arrived at the house, and of course he dropped me off while he made a few runs. I was pissed he came to get me just to have me cook his ass some dinner and for him to drop me off at home. That is what he wanted though, to keep tabs on me always, meanwhile he rips and runs the streets from hoe to hoe, from baby mama to baby mama. I made the meatloaf and chilled to occupy my time. In my feelings I wanted to hurt him somehow. He could not eat onions for whatever reason. In my cabinet I had some breadcrumbs with onions mixed in it and unnoticeable. I emptied more than half the can in the meatloaf and baked it.

When he got home, I had his plate made and ready to serve him as I did every time. I fed him. He smashed and did not notice the onions in the food. As time passed, while we chilled in the living room he started to complain. "Damn, I feel sick as fuck." He said while leaning over holding his stomach. I ignored him and continued to watch TV. "What the fuck was in that food?"

"I ate it, DBoy, and I am fine. It may be what you ate at your other bitch house." Of course, I had a slick comment to make.

"You got a smart ass—" And before he could finish, he was running to the bathroom with his hand over his mouth. As soon as he made it to the bathroom he dropped on his knees and started throwing up in the toilet. I did not help him, nor did I feel bad for the muthafucka. After he got himself together, he came in the living room talking shit. "So, your ass really just going to sit there while I was sick to my stomach, down on my knees?"

"Awe, now you need me, huh?" I rolled my eyes and went back to watching TV.

"You probably poisoned me, stupid bitch!" he said to me as he grabbed his keys and left.

One thing about me he needed to realize, I'm nobody's bitch, but I was THAT BITCH, and once I feel like you did something to me, I will hurt you the best way I can with no hard feelings or regrets. What is the saying? "I don't get mad, I get even." Yep, that was me all day.

Chapter 13
Up in Flames

Modeling was always something I wanted to do growing up. Many people told me I was pretty enough. Once I set my mind on something, then I will make a way to get whatever it is accomplished. I started looking up local modeling agencies, doing research to make sure it was no scamming going on. I finally found a modeling agency which was in Indianapolis, Indiana. I started the process to follow my dreams of becoming a model. I took some cute headshots and filled out the application for the agency. I was ready to follow my dreams. Being in the medical field was always something I wanted to do as well. So, I signed up for a phlebotomy class which lasted six weeks. Even though I was still at Defender I just was not happy there anymore. If I was going to work a 9 to 5, then I wanted it to be in the medical field. Something in demand, and a field making good money.

I was still without a car since someone stole my car off the side of the highway. Cheryl had a funny feeling about it. She kept telling me DBoy took my car so he could know and control my every move and that he was doing. I was depending on him to get everywhere I needed to go. Eventually he got tired of driving me around, so we went car shopping and as soon as I got me a car again, he was back to sending me to stings here and there. I had been at my job for a while and that was all they wanted, so DBoy paid my down payment and I was responsible for the monthly payments, which was cool. I was geeked to finally be in my own shit again. Depending on people to dictate when and how I moved just was not my thing.

It had been a few days since I've seen DBoy, even though we talked through text. He texted me asking me did I want to duck away tonight and get a room. When we went to the hotel it was always the same one a few minutes from my apartment. Of course, I told him yes. I packed my bags and waited for him but getting my hopes up was something I no longer did. One lesson I learned from him was setting people to high expectations always led to let downs. I wore my heart on my sleeve.

To my surprise he was there to pick me up 30 minutes later honking the horn like a wild man. I picked up my bags, made sure Tyson was cool, locked my door and left. We did what we always did. Chill, smoke, drank, fucked good, and passed out. DBoy could not get enough of this young, good pussy. He stayed between my legs every chance he got. Begging to fuck me in my ass was something he requested often, but my ass was a virgin and a finger was as good as it got. It was something about the makeup sex that night that made me go against my word and give up this ass. As good as it felt, it was something I could not get used to. I found it strange that he always made that request, but I never questioned him. The next day we went to breakfast and of course he dropped me off at home and went on his way.

I was accepted into the modeling agency. To my surprise, DBoy always supported me and made sure he was always with me when it came time for gigs and photoshoots. My first meeting he was right there with me. I met with the agent, filled out some paperwork, took some headshots, and started my portfolio. The meeting made me happy and I felt like finally something was being accomplished, something I always wanted to do.

DBoy had a homeboy who they called Buck, he was a known westside nigga and he knew Cheryl as well. He was an older cat who was getting money too. Well, he used to get money. Word around the hood was he was falling off. Buck and DBoy were tight since I came around on day one. I went to school with Buck's son, so he was way older than me. They were so tight they did hella shit together to get money. Buck even came over our house many times just to chill, or to buy some drugs from DBoy. He owned a club which was popping back in the day called Holmes. He was not doing shit with the building. As for DBoy, he was always trying to make a dollar.   He talked Buck into letting him rent the club out and making it a under 21 club. Buck agreed, and we started fucking it up every Saturday. He had one of the hottest djays every weekend, an off-duty sheriff as security, and I was the door girl. We charged $5 before ten and $10 after. DBoy started selling water, pop and chips too. I patted the girls down and took the money from everybody who came in. Buck was charging DBoy half of what he made to rent the building out. DBoy told me every chance I get, to stash some extra money away, and I did exactly what I was told to do. Every Saturday that shit was lit as fuck. In the city of Indianapolis, you must have a license to run a bar which they did not so we had to keep shit as discrete as we could. We did have alcohol in the back for us grown-ups.

The model agent called me for a gig she had set up in Chicago which she was providing transportation to and wanted me to join the tryouts. It was a big tryout for 7Up and Big Luster. It was something I had to be ready for within the next hour. I was determined and thirsty for success, so I made it happen. Me and eight other models along with our agent loaded up in her van and we were on a mini road trip. Once we got to the city, we went right to 7Up. It was a nice studio apartment that also had a photo booth set up as well. They also did advertisements for Colgate toothpaste. They had each of us line up as they looked at our portfolios. I was just getting started so mine was empty. By the end of each tryout we knew who made it, and I was not one of them. I was a little down and upset but was still excited that I got to experience something so awesome that I wanted to do all my life. On the way back home, we encountered a horrible snowstorm. I prayed the whole way we would make it back home. After a 2-hour drive turned into a 4-hour drive we finally made it back in town safely.

A week later I was done with my certificate for phlebotomy. Once again, I was proud of myself for another accomplishment I did on my own. It was a little ceremony, it wasn't much but DBoy made sure he supported me, and he was right there. Afterwards he took me out to eat and kept telling me how proud of me he was.

For a month straight, every Saturday we had the club jumping. This Saturday the police decided to fuck with us. As soon as I saw them pull up, I ran to the kitchen and told DBoy the police were outside, and they were about to walk in. He gave me all the drugs and the gun. I tucked the gun away and put the drugs in my fanny pack. As the police was walking in, I was slowly walking out. Looking like a kid anyway, I told them my ride was there and I needed to leave. I walked through the alley, watching my back, making sure the police did not pull up on me. I kept cutting through houses. I walked a nice minute away. I did not call DBoy's phone because I knew he was coming to look for me. As I continued pacing fast my phone rang.

"Baby, I got out. Where are you at?" he asked, still a little shook up.

"I am walking up Thirtieth Street towards Elmira." I slowed down walking because it was a streetlight and I did not want to bring no attention to me.

A few seconds later DBoy was pulling up, I hopped in and we headed to the apartment. He commended me for being so quick on my feet. "Daddy teaching you good." He said laughing but serious at the same time.

When we pulled up to the apartment everything was looking cool. DBoy was walking up behind me saying, "Damn, it smells like smoke."

I walked quickly in front of him and opened the door to the apartment, what I witnessed was a fucking nightmare. Smoke was coming from my kitchen. Me and DBoy both walked halfway in, but the smoke was too heavy for us to go in. We immediately set the alarms and went banging on every door in the apartment building to let them know it was a fire and they needed to get out.

Once we knocked on all the doors and everyone was out me and DBoy met on the sidewalk. I called 911, and DBoy was in my ear telling me he was leaving the scene and not to mention his name. Tyson was at the vet getting groomed which was a blessing. He had been there a few days. I kept cussing DBoy out to go get my baby, but he didn't. DBoy left the scene because of course it was all kinds of weed, cocaine, wet, and a few guns in there. We panicked and left the door open to the apartment and that made the fire spread instantly. Glass windows began to break out, my truck was covered in ashes. I was sick to my stomach as I sat and watched everything I worked hard for over the past years burn to ash.

The fire truck finally pulled up and they began jumping out the fire truck to fight the fire. I heard my name being called.

As I turned around it was DBoy hollering my name. "Rochelle, come on, let's go! Right now! I cannot just leave you here alone!"

Lost, confused and sick to my stomach I hopped in the car and we pulled off as they continued to fight the fire. As we pulled off, we saw the news channel pulling up.

DBoy was paranoid because of all the shit he had in the apartment. As I cried, he quickly tried to calm me down to talk to me. "It's cool, baby, we're gonna bounce back from this shit, but right now we got to make sure we don't get fucked up. You need to call Cheryl and her mom and let them know if anybody calls looking for you, they need to tell them they have not talked to you."

As I cleared my face off and calmed myself down, I made the phone calls he told me to make, then he made me turn off my phone. We went to his uncle's house on the northside of town and ducked off in his basement. As soon as we sat down, he turned on the news to see what was being said. It was breaking news, an apartment fire, but no more updates. As we sat on the couch watching TV, both exhausted we passed out cuddling.

After a few hours of sleep, my eyes were puffy, I was emotionally and mentally drained at this point. Reality hit me. All I had was the clothes on my back. Everything I worked so hard for was gone, all the memories and pictures I had of my mom were gone. I lost EVERYTHING in a matter of seconds, and my freedom was on the line because no telling what the police went in and found. I cut my phone back on, and I had about 30 messages from voicemails to text messages. Everybody calling to check on me. I had a missed call from the chief firefighter who stated he wanted to ask me a few questions regarding my apartment fire. I immediately called him back to see what it was he had to say over the phone before I went to meet with him.

"Hello, this is Rochelle returning your call in regard to an apartment fire," I said while DBoy listened in closely as well.

"Hello, this is Chief Dawson. I called to speak to you about the apartment fire which the lease is in your name. Are you available to meet me at the apartment today about one?"

"Yes, sir, I can be there at that time. Exactly what is it that we have to discuss?" I asked trying to see what he knew.

"Just ask a few questions about everything that took place that night. Is it something you are concerned about?" He asked.

"No, sir, I'm trying to get an understanding of all this right now. I am sorry, I will meet you at that time." I answered, still on the shaky side because I did not know what he knew or if they went in the house and found the drugs and guns.

DBoy was more worried about the police catching up to us than the loss he just took. See, being in the game you take a loss often, but what matters the most is how you bounce back. DBoy taught me that, and I knew in a few weeks he would have everything back together in no time.

Heading to the apartment DBoy told me, "I'm thinking a muthafucka broke in the apartment, took all my shit and set it on fire to cover up them breaking in."

I had no reply, I felt like at this point he had some idea of what the fuck was going on. We pulled up to the apartment to meet him. The cars that were sitting in front of my apartment was covered by ashes from the fire. We met the man outside, we sat in his car to talk while DBoy was in his own car. He did not want his name on or in nothing.

"Okay, Ms. Brown, we are still looking into this fire to see exactly what the cause was. I am sorry for the loss of all your personal belongings, but you still have your life. I have a few questions I need to ask you if that is okay with you?" He asked with his pen and paper in hand.

"Yes, sir, that is fine." As I felt a tear fall down my face.

"Okay, we have already gotten statements from witnesses. Can you tell me what you were doing the night of the fire?" He was ready to write some shit down.

"Yes, sir, I was at an under twenty-one party. After the party I came right home." I told him. DBoy always told me when being asked questions by investigators to give less detail as possible.

"Who all lives here with you?" He waited on my reply so he could write more details down.

"Nobody, sir. Just me and my dog who was at the vet getting groomed." I felt like I just committed a crime answering all those questions.

"Are you currently feuding with anyone who would want to harm you?"

"No, sir. I work and come home. I mind my business, sir." I replied telling him somewhat of the truth.

"Was there any suspicious activity when you arrived at your apartment?" he asked.

"No, sir." I replied dryly.

"Okay, I will return to the office, sift through what has been learned at the fire scene, witness statements, fire department response records, and investigation of the fire to come up with a reason for this fire." He told me as the meeting came to an end. It was short and sweet.

Me and DBoy went to the apartment leasing house to meet with them next. The police were not involved so he was cool with being present. The leasing agent took us to see the inside of the apartment. It was absolutely nothing left, no walls, and everything I had worked hard for was completely gone. All my pictures of Sandal and me as a child were gone. That pain hit different because I had nobody I could reach out to, to send me more pictures of me as a child and none of my mother. The springs to the bed was about the only thing that it made out. The Pyrex glass DBoy used to cook his crack in was sitting on the floor. DBoy swiftly picked it up and tucked it in his coat. I did not have no rental insurance at all. I had to leave from inside the apartment because seeing all my shit gone to ashes hurt me, tears would not stop falling. DBoy stayed inside looking around to see if he could find anything that made it through the fire.

As I walked down the steps, I heard a spark. As I screamed and ran down the steps DBoy came to check on me. "What, baby?" he yelled so concerned.

"Shit is still sparking, hurry up and come from up there." I told him, scared because I did not know what the fuck was going on, plus I was just ready to get away from there.

We went back to the leasing office and spoke with the office manager. They had me another one-bedroom apartment but they needed a few days to get it ready for move in. The apartments bought us a hotel room until our apartment was done and ready for move in.

We went to the room where he told me he was going to stay with me until we got settled in the new apartment, and that he was also trying to figure out exactly what could have happened for the fire to happen. After we brainstormed, we went right to sleep, still exhausted mentally and physically, as well as still wondering if and what they found in the apartment as far as the drugs and guns, and still wondering if the police were going to come knocking on the hotel door and lock us up. Normally sex would have been the first thing we did once we checked into the room but this time it was different, that was the furthest thing on our minds. We got checked in the room about 7PM and we slept the rest of the day and night.

Beep beep beep beep! My alarm went off and it was time to go to work for the first day since the fire. DBoy took me to get a few outfits so I could at least go to work looking presentable until I could get my "closet" back to how it was. DBoy lost about $12,000 total from the fire between his cocaine, weed, wet and cash money. Still in the clear from the police but we were still a little worried.

Warning Before Destruction

Word had got out about my apartment catching fire and me losing everything. Cheryl and her family were a big help. Sandal's brother sent me a gift card for $500.00, and people started donating little things to me as well. I was referred to a place called "Burn Victims' Unit" which was like a Goodwill for people who have lost things in a fire, but it was all free stuff. When I arrived to work all my coworkers were asking me questions about what happened. Word got around the building quick, that lead to more and more donations from people.

Chapter 14
Another Beginning

I was in my new one-bedroom apartment cleaning up and getting ready to move in what little things I had collected over the last few weeks. Taking a load in, I heard a man's voice say, "Excuse me, miss. Do you need any help?" It was the apartments' maintenance man.

"No, I got it. Thanks though." I said as I started moving toward the house.

He came closer to me saying, "I overheard in the leasing office your apartment caught fire from cooking cocaine in there. You might want to cover your tracks."

I stopped right in my tracks. "I work daily so I don't know where they would get that lie from." I covered shit up.

"I am not sure what they are doing but just make sure you watch your back." He gave me a heads up. I took heed to what he said and immediately called DBoy to let him know what the latest news was from the leasing office.

The weekend came back around, and as always, we were back at Homers. During the day DBoy would hustle out of there, have niggas gambling, and even sell dinners sometimes. The OG's people had the daytime and the weekends while the youngsters had the club on Saturday nights. *"If the outcome is income,"* was DBoy's favorite saying, and he was getting it by any means, especially after the loss he just took from the house fire. The club was filled from wall to wall. All the kids would be throwing up their hood, the girls dancing all on the boys and having a good time. From time to time DBoy would go out on the dance floor and fuck around with the kids. He had to play security most of the nights. At the door, as always, I could see who was coming in or leaving out, I was checking on a girl when a woman walked through the door kind of fast.

As I looked up, me and her made eye contact. I'll be damned, it was that bitch Shae walking in and heading toward DBoy on the dance floor. She got to him on the dance floor, whispered something to him and they walked off to the kitchen. I kept my cool, but I thought, *I'll give this bitch a few minutes in that kitchen and if they don't come out, I am going to act a fool.* A few seconds later she was walking out, sticking some money in her pockets. She walked out and I rolled my eyes at her. As bad as I wanted to knock her ass out as she walked by me I didn't. I could hear DBoy now talking all kinds of shit because I beat the fuck out of his baby mama. I was learning to control myself and trying to grip the concept that not every action requires a reaction.

DBoy was on the dance floor playing security like he always did when a fight broke out, and before you knew it DBoy and Buck was snatching the boys up and carrying them to the door. The youngster DBoy had was trying to fight him once they knocked on the doorway. Now as I told you DBoy was crazy and he did not play no games when it came to disrespect. He'd just come home with busted knuckles from knocking a nigga out for stealing from him. Confused I ran outside to try and calm him down, and before you knew it the little boy tried to run up on DBoy again, he pushed him down so hard he fell. As the little boy sat there, I got DBoy back in the building. He finally calmed down and was back to business.

The weekend was over, and it was time to get back to work. As I was packing my belongings up to go to lunch, my supervisor came up to me tapping me on my shoulder. "Can you please come in the conference room really quick?"

"Sure." I was confused as to what was happening. See, I loved having my own money but hated working a 9 to 5 to get the check, so losing my job was the last thing I needed. I was already on probation for my attendance, always calling in or late fucking around with DBoy most of the times.

As I walked into the conference room it was filled with the president of the company, my whole team and few other people from different departments. Cheryl had quit there to focus on law school. I followed my supervisor to the front of the room where the president was standing with a microphone.

"Okay, as everyone knows from the emails that were sent, Rochelle suffered an extreme loss from a house fire. Rochelle has been great to us here, reaching her weekly goals and going above and beyond for others. We, as a family, had to all come together in this time of need for you. This is for you." He handed me an envelope.

I slowly opened it, wondering what in the world is this. I finally got it opened and pulled out the paper that was inside. To my surprise, it was a check in the amount of $1,500.00. Tears started rolling down my face as I looked at the check and gave the President a hug. I then wiped my face and began to speak. "I just want to say thank you to each one of you who donated. I am so blessed to be a part of such a great company, and family. I am going to buy me some more furniture TODAY! Also, thanks to everyone who reached out and donated things other than money. Thanks everyone so much."

I called DBoy and told him what had just happened. He was excited for me as well. When I got off that day, I went right to do what I said I was going to do. I purchased a living room set, living room tables, and a dining room table. It was a place that sells "Apartments to go" and I went there to get the hook up. I was overly excited and blessed that my job looked out for me the way they did.

Me and DBoy were fucking like rabbits, every free chance we got, he was on me or I was on him, no matter where we were. As bad as I wanted a baby to fill the void in my life, I didn't, because as my nigga always reminded me, if I got pregnant he was going back home to Shae. I was not on birth control, but he pulled out every time. I started to think I couldn't have kids as much as we fucked and I wasn't pregnant yet. I was on birth control from my sophomore year until a few months ago. One of our fierce nights we had our first scare.

"Damn, I'm, I'm cumming!" He yelled while still deep inside of me. Yelp, he came inside of me for the first time. He laid on me for a few seconds before he jumped up yelling "Go piss and push that shit out. You got to go to the pharmacy in the morning and get that Morning After, Plan B shit. That shit was so good that I couldn't fall out, girl." He slapped me on my ass. The next morning, he gave me some money and I went to get the pill from the CVS pharmacy. I put the pill in my purse and kept going on about my day. I did not want to take it because if I was pregnant, I wanted the baby. When I talked to DBoy, that was the first thing he asked me.

"You take that pill already?" He asked.

Without hesitation I replied "Yes!"

DBoy's cousin from Louisville and his woman came to visit us. Partying and going out was not our thing, unless we were at Homer's. They were only in town for the day so we decided to just chill, smoke, drink and talk at our house. It was a good time as it was the last time. DBoy and his cousin left us at the house while they went to the liquor store and to make a few moves as he called it. We sat and talked as if we had known each other for years. I trusted her a little bit so I felt like I could open to her.

"So, DBoy nutted all in me a few days ago, he sent me to get the morning after pill but I ain't taking that shit." I bragged about it.

"Girl give it to me, I need to take it. Shit, I was sure going first thing in the morning when we get back home." So, I did just that.

"Okay, this has to stay our secret, even though I don't think I am pregnant." I said laughing.

"Bet, I won't say shit girl." She assured me.

The fellas came back and we continued to enjoy our night as if nothing never happened. They left late that night as we went to bed. DeBoy had sentencing in the morning for this case and he needed to be rested.

The next morning he was headed to court and of course, I was not allowed to go. I kissed him as he left, and I went to work. He finally called me, letting me know they put him on house arrest and he would be doing that at his mama's house, which was 10 minutes from the apartment. I was happy because every night I knew where he would be. His mama was a mean grumpy old lady who always stayed in his room. She would speak and hold short convos but that was all. Living in his mama's house was also his grandma, and uncle, which were cool people. Even though he was on house arrest, he was able to come out at night. He told the people that he worked a 3rd shift job. He told the house arrest people he had 2 jobs, so he was always out in the streets, spending most of his time at Homers. I could not understand how he had so much freedom, but I guess it was not for me to understand. The way he had his time set up, he was able to still run Homer's all day and night. DBoy always told me that the number one reason for homicide is because a muthafucka was being nosey. Never ask no questions.

Warning Before Destruction

The less I knew, the better but he was showing me a lot. I was still making his moves for him while he was on house arrest during the hours he could not come out. He was not letting nothing stop his grind.

DBoy had a female cousin named Nakia. She just got home from doing time for her nigga, but it was also her birthday and she wanted a party at Homer's. Even though DBoy was a rough ass nigga, he still had a soft side to him and helping his people was a subject that brought that out of him. So, he told her yes and got everything together for her party.

It was a nice crowd of people. She had a friend named Stacee, who was eyeing my nigga all night. After a few hours, she was sloppy drunk. Her and DBoy danced together but I was not tripping over that. Hell, I knew he was my man and he was going home with me. As long as the bitch didn't get disrespectful, I was cool. He walked toward me holding his arms out and dancing, I fell in his arms as we danced. I was having a great time. Most of the time, I sat behind the bar being the boss bitch that I was. DBoy went to the kitchen and Stacee followed behind him laughing and giggling. One song played, a second song played, a third and a fourth song played, and they were still in the kitchen. I took a deep breath before I got up and walked back there. I walked into her whispering in his ear.

"Why is she all in your face and has been all night?" I pointed at the bitch walking closer and closer to him.

"Man chill out." He said laughing and pushing me back. I felt like he was showing out in front of this bitch and taking me as a joke.

"I will beat this bitch ass and yours!" I yelled as I grabbed a hand full of dreads, wrapped them around my hand and pulled him out of the kitchen through the club and outside. His dreads were down to his ass, and I made sure I gripped them tight. Once again, I let my anger get the best of me. When we got outside, he was still laughing, making me more and more mad.

"You think this shit is a fucking joke? I'm not a fucking game, nor are my muthafucking feelings." I yelled as I kept hitting and pushing him. At this point, the whole club was outside. Everybody was just watching as shit got more and more intense between us. I pushed him and he stumbled. Shit was not funny to him now.

"Now, you are doing too fucking much out here, calm down." He yelled as he pushed me with what seemed like all his might. I feel back, I hit my head on a rock and hit my rib on a big brick. I got up in so much pain. His phone was on the ground, I picked it up and threw it as far as I could. He came toward me and I started swinging. I turned around to run away but before I got too far away, he came from behind me and pushed me again. I fell on my face. I rolled over and as soon as I did, I felt a jab to my mouth. I tried to get back up but was too weak to do so. He put his hands around my neck and squeezed tight.

Chapter 15
Torn and Battered

"Bitch, I will fucking kill you out here. You better get your shit and get the fuck away from around here Rochelle and I mean it!" He said full of anger.

"Everybody get back in the muthafucking building!" He told the crowd. Nobody helped me or even attempted to. I felt like my life was about to end. My face was full of tears as I was crying and hyperventilating. I found my car keys and went to sit in my car. I turned the light on and all I saw was blood. My knee was bleeding, and my pants were all torn in the knees. I could taste blood so I licked my lips only to feel that my two front teeth were cracked, and more than half was gone from BOTH of my front teeth. I had a huge gash in my lip which was gushing out blood too. I started to panic and cry even more still sitting outside in the car. The crowd was walking out to be nosey at this point as DBoy walked back in. Stacee even came out and I yelled.

"You're a stupid bitch, If that's what you want then you can have him." I pulled off. Even though DBoy was drunk and I put my hands on him first, I was in awe that he just beat the shit out of me. I drove to the nearest gas station and got out to get me some napkins to stop the bleeding.

"Damn baby girl, you cool?" A man yelled as I was walking into the store.

"Yeah, I am good." I kept walking just wanting some tissue to slow down the bleeding and to get home.

"Call the police!" Another man yelled.

"Noooooo, please. Don't do that. I am okay." The police were not what I wanted to do. I looked at myself in the light at the gas station and I looked crazy. I looked exactly like what just happened, I got my ass beat. I ran in to get the napkins and quickly made my way back to my truck. Still crying, I finally arrived home, which seemed like it was the longest ride ever. I pulled up at home and ran into my house. DBoy had a key so I locked both locks and put the chain on it. I went into the bathroom and ran the water, making my hand a cup. I sipped the water and gargled. After I got my face cleaned up, I took my clothes off to see what else was bleeding. The pain I was feeling in my back and ribs was unbearable. The cut I had on my head was bleeding too. I was in so much pain I just wanted to clean myself up and pass out. While I was getting myself together, my phone was blowing up off the hook. It was DBoy but I had no intentions on answering any of his calls. I knew he was on house arrest so he would not be popping up. Finally, I was all cleaned up. I was headed to my bed, leaning over and barely walking from the pain I was in.

BOOM. BOOM. BOOM. It was 3 bangs on my door. I didn't ask who it was. I slowly crept to the peephole.

"Rochelle, baby. Please let me in, baby." The man's voice pleaded and cried. I looked through the peephole and sure enough it was DBoy.

"Bryce, your curfew is coming. Please just go home." I yelled through the door.

"Baby no, I can't. I need to see you. Please just open the door for me. I am sorry Rochelle." He was still pleading.

"Nooooo, and if you killed my baby, I'm going to make your life a living hell." I told him, not even sure if I was pregnant or not. "Get the fuck away from me please. I hate you for this." I told him, barely yelling because of the pain I was in.

"Just please, let me in to talk to you. Please baby. Please. I will kick this door down if I have to." His voice was cracking.

"Kick my fucking door in and I am calling the police on you." I said hoping that would get him to leave. He was not giving up. Five minutes later, he was still banging and crying. I gave in and opened the door. I knew his curfew was coming and I did not want him to miss it and risk getting locked up again. As soon as he came in, he fell to my feet, crying, begging and pleading even more. I was disgusted with him at this point. There was nothing he could say or do to change that at this point. His trap phone rung because his daily phone he used was the one I threw. It was the same bitch that was just in his face at the club. He wouldn't answer so I took his phone. As soon as I said hello, she hung up. Her number was stored in his phone. I was unsure if that was something that been occurred, or it just occurred. I was too exhausted to fuss and fight, so I gave him his phone back and told him to leave my fucking house. It was 1:55 am and his curfew was 2:00 am.

"I love you, Rochelle. I am so sorry baby, I swear I am. I wish I didn't have to leave you right now. I don't know what came over me." He cried as he walked out the door.

I slammed the door and went to lay in my bed. I held my pillow tight and cried myself to sleep. I slept off and on for a few hours but the pain I was in was too much to sleep through.

The next morning I had missed calls from Cheryl and her mother, but I did not answer. From the way they were calling, it made me think they knew what was going on. This is a secret I had to keep to myself because If I did not leave him then it would cause a whole different issue.

When I woke up, I called the dentist as well as my doctor to make emergency appointments. Thank God they had openings, or I was going to be sitting in the house. I was a model and I could not be walking around with chipped teeth. Then, I had to call my supervisor to let her know I could not make it in today.

BOOM. BOOM. BOOM. I creeped to the door, not asking who it was. I looked out the peephole. It was Baba Musa. I did not answer and was confused on how Cheryl even knew anything about what happened to send him to do a welfare check on me. I mean she did know a lot of people, but I was unsure at the party who would have called her. After Babe Musa did not get an answer, he left. 10 minutes later, he was back with the maintenance man. They banged on the door again, but I was in my bed and still had the chain attached so they could not get in. I was sure he knew I was in there. They left and did not come back. I did not know what the protocol was for that type of call, but I was hoping they did not send the police to kick my door in.

45 minutes later, I heard a bang on the door and the door being opened but the chain was on.

"Rochelle, open up baby. It's me!"

It was 8:00 am and DBoy was not supposed to be out until 12:00 pm. Confused, and knowing I needed him to pay for my teeth because I could not use my insurance, I slowly walked to the door. I slowly opened it. I was dreading seeing his fucking face. He hugged me.

"Ouch," I hollered because he squeezed me too tight.

"Man, I am so sorry. Look at you. Did you call the dentist?" He was acting concerned but I could not give in so easy this time. I had to play hard.

"Yes, my doctor appointment is at 10:00 am and my dentist appointment is at 1:00 pm. I hope you cleared your schedule to be at both." I replied in smartest way I could.

"Calm down man, damn. Let's just lay down and let me hold you." He lightweight snapped on me, then calmed down fast. I did not reply. I just limped to my room and laid down, and he followed right behind me. He laid behind me and held me. Not saying a word, but I was cool with that. I really had no conversation for the nigga. He tried to ease his hands under my robe. I was in too much pain to even have on clothes. I stopped him before he could get too far. I was not going out like that. I was not turned on right now. I had a lot on my mind, hell I wouldn't even get wet right now.

It was finally time to get up and start getting ready for my appointments. I had very little strength, but I needed to take a shower. Finally, I was able to take a shower and get dressed. In the meantime, Cheryl and her family kept blowing up my phone. I had no intentions to talk to anyone until I was back to myself. As they called, I just ignored the calls. Plus, discussing anything to them that happened in front of DBoy was going to lead to another issue. He did not like people in his business as he said, and he felt like I was twenty-one and too grown to be telling my mama what happened. I had nobody I could vent to and trust they would not judge me if I had plans on going back to him. Love is a powerful ass drug, and to make it so bad, I was addicted to a love that treated me like shit. Before we arrived in the doctor's office, we stopped to get a few surgical masks to hide my teeth until I got to the dentist.

"Rochelle." The nurse came out yelling my name. I got up and walked to follow her and DBoy was right behind me. She weighed me in and sat us in the room, asking the normal questions to get a chart prepared for the doctor. She made me pee in a cup for a pregnancy test. She finally asked what happened, and I had to lie and tell her I got into a fight at the club with some girls I did not know. After they finally examined me, she told me I had a mild concussion and a bruised rib. She also told me my pregnancy test was negative. She prescribed me some Xanax for my nerves and told me to take some over the counter pain pills. She also gave me a note to be off from work for a week to relax and heal. All DBoy could do was shake his head. I tried so hard not to cut my eyes at him or show any anger towards him. I did not want them to think he had anything to do with it at all.

We got my meds from the pharmacy and we were off to the dentist. My teeth were so sensitive and sore I could not eat nor drink, so I would have to wait to take my pills. Once we got there and I checked in, they did X-rays on my mouth to see what they had to fix. Of course, I was asked what happened and once again I told them the same lie as I did the doctor's office. Coming back in with my results from the X-ray, the dentist spoke.

"This is major, Rochelle. We got some major fixing to do here. I can give you a temporary fix for about $300 or I can give you a permanent fix for about $1,500."

I had to take that up with DBoy, who was in the waiting room because this was coming out of his pocket. "Give me a second and let me go see." I told her as I went to check with him.

"Nah, just get a temporary fix and we'll see who else can do what."

I told the dentist to give me the temporary fix as DBoy had told me to do. After a forty-five min procedure, I had temporary front teeth. The whole time all I could do was replay that whole night in my head repeatedly. I was still in shock that this nigga just really fucked me up like that. My mouth was numb so I still had to wait to eat. I had to wait longer and longer to take the pills my doctor prescribed me. The temporary fix was a cool fix but I was ready to hurry up and get my permanent teeth so it would be done and paid for.

After all of that running, I was ready to eat something soft as I was told, take my Xanax pills and rest. DBoy dropped me off at home, made sure I was comfortable and tucked into bed. I finally decided to call Cheryl and let her know that I was okay and tried to twist the story up as much as I could so she would not hate DBoy no more what she already hated him. When I told her about my teeth, she was pissed bringing up how she paid good money to get my braces because my teeth were so gapped. She said somebody that was at the party told her what happened.

"I had to work, and you know I can't miss no more days so I sent dad to check on you."

After 30 minutes of hearing her mouth, she finally told me she would be over when she got off to see me. I knew that was coming. She always called the love she gives me tough love but that was not what I called it. Especially putting me out a day after graduation because I did not do what she wanted me to do. Yelp, I was still holding on to anger and bitterness in my heart towards her.

Chapter 16
Boy Bye

DBoy was still on house arrest. After that incident, he was nice to me for a while before he started back to his asshole ways. I started staying the night often at his mother's house with him. He had his own room and a futon we slept on. Still the same as he was when he was free, he did not want to lay up under me EVERY NIGHT. I guess he was sneaking bitches in and out. If I was under him and knowing most of his moves, I cared less how we slept. I still had my apartment, which I only had a few more months left in the lease there before it expired.

DBoy and Shae were done, at least that was what he told me, and what did I do? Believe his ass. This man had my mind so gone it was sickening. It was like he put a spell on me that had me deeply in love with this no-good ass nigga. I could not leave him alone, nope not even after he just beat my ass giving me a bruised rib, mild concussion and fake teeth in the front of my mouth. DBoy wanted me to get a house since the lease was almost up anyway, and he wanted to move a lot of his stuff to my place.

My apartment was too small, so he told me to look for a house to rent. At this time, the house he was rebuilding when we first met was just sitting half ass done. The whole house was gutted out. Once he got the case, it slowed down everything for him. Plus, since his main worker who was working for him and getting the plugs at the store had snitched on him, he was stuck with no plug.

He already talked to his brother who agreed to take over the lease for the last few months, which included paying the electric bill and rent. He was a young street dude following in the tracks of his brother, so I trusted him to take care of my shit. Plus, he had his bitch moving in with him. I didn't know the girl, we went on a few double dates but that was about it. I expected her as a woman to be on him as it should be to keep a roof over their head and keep the bills paid.

Me and DBoy started looking for houses together. He wanted me to move closer to his mom's house since that was where he was doing his house arrest, which was on the west side of Indianapolis. After a few days of looking, we found a two-bedroom, one bathroom, attached car garage, fireplace, huge fenced in backyard with a shed that was empty and available to the renters. It was $750.00 a month. Something Cheryl always instilled in me was when getting a place to live with or without a nigga always make sure you can handle the rent by yourself. $750 a month was something I could handle on my own, so I applied for the house and I got approved.

DBoy paid the rent up for a few months on the house when we first moved in so that would not be an issue. Man, I was happy. That meant more time and stability and in my own place. One thing about fucking with the dope man was he always had stings that would do whatever he asked of them. Of course, to move from the apartment to the house, I only had to worry about getting a few things and transporting in my truck. The stings would come and do anything from fixing shit, to bathing the dogs, training the dogs, cleaning and beheading his fish fresh from the water, to fixing our cars. The following day, DBoy was out on a work pass, He moved all his shit from Shae's house to mine. He had big screen TV's, his motorcycle, a lot of his clothes and shoes. Something happened between him and Shae because he was finally moving all his shit to my place, even his Pitts. Since DBoy was on house arrest, he made me the babysitter for his kids when he had a pass out from his house arrest. Even Shae's kids started coming over more often as well. I still had my dog Tyson, which I kept in the house, but DBoy just brought me another Yorkie which I named Princess. He kept his Pitts chained up on the fence in the big backyard. We had to keep my dog far away from his because they were so damn aggressive and mean. He set up shop in the barn for his area where he trained his dogs by having them run on the treadmill for hours. After my first dog fight with him, I made sure it was my last. I could not stomach that shit. Even though he paid the rent up at our new house, he still had to go home to his mother's house when he was not on a pass for his house arrest. I was still staying the night with him at his mama house, only if we were not arguing or he was not on some bullshit I was there cooking dinner for him and his whole family that lived in the house. His mom, grandma, and uncle.

DBoy would go to our house and post up on every break he got from house arrest. One day while sitting outside not the porch, he called me. Fuck the fact I was at work, whenever he called, I better answer or he was going to cuss me out. Regardless if I was at work or anywhere else, my phone better not have gone unanswered. Once again, I covered up by saying "He is just training me up to be a woman." I was just young and dumb.

"Hold on while I go to the breakroom from my desk." I walked away fast to the breakroom.

"What's up baby?" I said as I got a chair and sat down in the breakroom.

"So, Shae is riding by the house, I'm sitting on the porch and the bitch just drove by." He was saying as he sounded like he was surprised. Wasn't no telling how she got my address, but I was not liking the fact that she knew where I laid my head at.

"She gone fuck around and get her ass whooped if she keeps playing with me, I just hope you ain't playing both sides in this situation because that is going to make shit more conflicted. You better call and check your bitch." I told him with much aggression in my voice so he would know I was not fucking around. Since I been fucking with this man, this bitch has been all out of pocket.

"I am, I was just calling you to give you a heads up on that. Call me when you go on lunch." We both hung the phone up.

It was finally time for me to get my teeth permanently put in by DBoy's dentist who he went to often. When I got up out of the chair, I was feeling more confident in myself with permanent teeth. DBoy had to pay $3,500 to get my two front teeth fixed. I was not feeling bad at all about him spending it. He kept making slick comments about if I kept my hands to myself, he would not be spending all this extra money. My teeth were back to normal.

I had to call my model agent and let her know I was okay and ready to get back to what I loved. I told my agent the same lying ass story I told the doctor and dentist office. After I explained my story to her, she started to fill me in on a model bootcamp she was sending me to, as well as a Paul Mitchell Hair Show she wanted me to go to the calling for. She gave me the details for where I needed to be. I wrote it down in my calendar and we both hung up.

Since I got my ass kicked by DBoy, Cheryl started calling me more often and checking on me. I was still taking my

Xanax as needed. Most of the time it was when DBoy made me shitty. The pills made me so high I would forget about anything stressing me out. In the last few months, I lost so much weight everyone started to think I was on drugs. I was stressed the fuck out and not eating. It was a constant emotional roller coaster with DBoy.

"Rochelle?" Cheryl called as I picked up the phone.

"Yes, ma?" I replied low. I was upset because DBoy was not answering my calls.

"What are you doing? You want to go out to eat with me?" She asked to my surprise.

"Ummmm sure." I replied, unsure if I wanted to go because I just took Xanax, and I knew I would be nodding off. This was not an invite I got often so I took her up on the offer and met her at Applebee's. It had been a minute since I've seen her, but she hugged me tight and whispered in my ear.

"No matter what you think, I love you and that will never change." I smiled and hugged her back. I cannot lie, it felt kind of good hearing her say that to me. I did not have an appetite and shortly after I sat down, my pill started to kick in. I started nodding off like I knew I would. Then of course when Cheryl saw me nod off, she would call my name and talk her shit about how I need to stop taking them. She did not let me drive home, she drove me out west to my place. As soon I got in the door, I passed out sleep on my bed. I had nobody to talk to. I knew everybody would judge me and call me stupid because leaving him was not in my plans no time soon. Stephanie and Cheleste were still hanging tight. I became the outcast and hardly talked to them. Patricia already had a strong feeling towards my situation so venting to her was not an option. Cheryl always had to preach to me and I wasn't hearing her mouth or giving her the opportunity to say I told you so. So, taking pills was the next way to handle the bullshit I was going through. All I really had was me and DBoy and he was one of the reasons for my stress so venting to him didn't make no sense. It seemed like the more I bitched and whined about his lying sneaky ways, the worse he got. Playing cool with the hoes in the beginning was easy, but once feelings got involved I wanted all that shit to come to an end bad. Though that was what I wanted, I knew I was not going to get it from DBoy.

Like always when I spent the night with DBoy over his mama's house, I got up, got dressed for work, kissed my nigga goodbye and headed to my house to let my dogs out before I went to work for the day. This morning I saw an unfamiliar car with tints sitting down the street. One thing I always did was check my surroundings. It was a person in the driver seat but the way the morning sun was shining in my eyes, I could not see who was in the car. I continued to walk to my car as I kept an eye on the black on black car. The car followed me home, which was five minutes from DBoy's mama's house. I was already running behind getting ready for work and could not be late, so I did not have time to play with this car. As I pulled up at home in my driveway, the car pulled directly in front of my house. As I looked, the bitch jumped out of her car at the same time as I did. I had my keys in my hand ready to stab her ass if she tried to touch me. As soon as she got to the end of my driveway she yelled.

"I just want to know if you were over there for Bryce?"

It was Shae. This bitch had the nerve to really follow me. The last few times I saw her out, I let her ride without an ass whopping, but now you feel bold enough to come on my property asking me about my man, and you followed me. Oh yeah, I had to give her what she really wanted. An ass whooping for stalking me and the truth about who I was. She had a black pouch which I thought it was a gun. Walking up my driveway slowly while we were exchanging words.

"Listen here, SHAE, we have had too many run ins for you to not know who the fuck I am." I told her straight up. At this point, I was not worried about DBoy finding out how bad I beat his baby mama's ass for following me home and walking up on me.

"Awe, so you the one he's been fucking around with for all this time? And you know my name, huh?"

"Bitch? Are you illiterate? I think you need to skip your ass on down that road somewhere."

"Or what? What you gon' do boo. From what I hear, my baby daddy got you on a tight ass leash."

"Shae, I won't repeat myself!"

"Girl, please." She smirked, finally stepping towards me. I realized the pouch in her hand was her phone case, so I was in the clear to whoop her ass.

I punched her right in her face and it was a brawl from there. After the first punch I threw, I kept giving them to her so she would not have a chance to get me. We fumbled in the grass as she was trying to hit me back. We fell to the ground and I got on top of her, letting her know who the fuck I was.

"Bryce is my nigga and been my nigga for years." I yelled as I kept punching her. The neighbor was a younger black man who happened to see us fighting. He came and pulled me off her, letting her free to get up and sneak me a few times. Another neighbor heard all the commotion and came running out his front door. He grabbed Shae as she was punching me, and I was kicking her because the man had my arms pulled back behind my head.

"I've been with him for 4 years and I have kids by him, so my spot is secure, you little bitch." She said as her lip was leaking blood.

They finally got Shae in her car and she pulled off. I was on fire and shitty that the neighbor grabbed me off her. I had a few years' worth of ass whoopings for her bitch ass. She did get me good a few times when the man was holding me back, but it was all good because if I got to her again, I swear I was going to kill her. I felt like at this point DBoy was still fucking with this bitch for her to come doing all of that. I needed answers from him, and I needed them fast and not slow. After finally calming down in my living room and the bitch was gone as well as the neighbors, I finally called DBoy.

"Hello," he answered still half asleep, like he was when I just left him.

"So, your weak ass baby mama, Shae, decided to follow me from your house to around here, and yes I did beat her the fuck up for following me and walking up on me. You have to be telling this bitch something for her to be so deep in her feelings. She sat outside your mama's house to see who was there." I was yelling at him through the phone.

"I haven't been telling her nothing. You already know I do not do this extra ass shit." He lightweight snapped on me like I did something wrong. Hell, all I did was protect myself which I had every right to do so.

"Your bitch followed me, and you have the balls to snap on me for defending myself?" I was even more pissed at this point for him tripping on me like I was in the wrong.

"Man, I don't know what the fuck is going on, I am in the bed sleep. I am just saying you know I do not do this shit at all.

I will call you back. Let me call and see what the fuck is going on." The phone hung up.

After I hung up with him, I called my supervisor to let her know that I would not be in today. She told me I would have to have a meeting with her when i got back for my attendance. My performance was great. Every week I would get the bonus, but it was my attendance I was fucking up on. It was just too much that just happened for me, so fast and unexpectedly with Shae this morning. It was no way I could walk into work like everything was okay and be focused.

DBoy never called me back, nor was he answering his phone. So, I drove back around to his mama's house. I'll be damned, this crazy bitch went back to DBoy's mama's house and was outside causing a scene, yelling at the top of her lungs and pointing her finger all in his face. I kept driving because I did not want to cause an issue at his mama's and then I will no longer be able to go back over there I was sure. His mama did not play no games at all. I knew my mouth and his mama's mouth was going to lead to a whole different situation and I did not want to end up beating that old lady's ass.

That sneaky, you got to be quiet sex was the best. That's how me and DBoy had to be at his mama's house. Even though he was a grown ass man and paying bills there, it was just out of respect for his mom and grandma. The last few weeks DBoy had been nutting in me like crazy. Mother's Day

2008 after we woke up at his mama's house, it was time for his pass out to start. We got up and went to our house. The house was a mess from me just running in and out, grabbing clothes and going to lay up under DBoy. When I got in the house, I got right to cleaning my house. A few minutes later, I was feeling so sick to my stomach. I laid down for a second. As soon as I did, my head started spinning, I got up to run to the toilet. Within the last few weeks, I have thrown up a few mornings. As I laid over the toilet feeling like shit and throwing up nothing but stomach acid, DBoy peeped his head in the bathroom saying, "I'll be right back."

As he left through the door, I was in shock that he left me the way he did while I was sick. I finally got myself together and went to lay down on my bed. To my surprise, he was right back. He came in the room and handed me a pregnancy test. As soon as I got the strength to get up, I went to the bathroom and pissed on the stick. I sat it on the counter and went back to lay down while the shit processed. DBoy was anxious to know what the results were.

"Fuckkkkkkkk, I fucking knew it!" DBoy yelled as loud as he could.

"What is it?" I got up and ran to the bathroom.

"You are pregnant, man. Fuck!" He yelled again. He was pissed. He did not want me to have this baby. The first thing that rolled off his tongue was "Are you going to get an abortion?"

"Damn, I mean this shit hit me so unexpectedly. Can I have a minute to think on some shit?" I asked him.

"What the fuck you mean a minute to think on it. What the fuck is there to think about? That sounds like you are trying to keep this baby. I told you if you had a baby I am gone, and I meant that shit. Shit is sweet with no kids right now between me and you." He was talking louder than normal but not screaming, pacing the house. He was acting like he didn't know what happens when a man nuts in a woman. He was so pissed that he grabbed his keys and left, like he always did me when I made him mad. That was nothing new. My feelings were hurt. I laid in the bed and cried my heart out. As I held my stomach, all I could think about is what I just found out. I was pregnant. I was carrying a life inside of me. I knew shit was about to get real between me and DBoy because he did not want this baby at all. I knew he was going to make me choose between him or my unborn child. I cried myself to sleep.

I woke up a few hours later and found the strength to get up and put some clothes on to start celebrating Mother's Day at Cheryl's house. DBoy had not called me since he left earlier. I got dressed and was headed to Cheryl's house. Patricia was there and I had to tell somebody, so I called her when I pulled up and told her to come outside. I had the pregnancy test in my purse because shit just seemed so not real to me. I was sure she was not going to have nothing positive to say about the situation, but I needed to tell somebody. I had no plans on telling Cheryl I was pregnant until later. I was sure it was not going to be nothing good coming from her. Patricia came outside and hopped in my truck. I pulled out the test and the first thing she said was "Oh lord, now you are pregnant by this crazy ass nut, Rochelle?"

"Yeah but don't tell nobody yet." I said making sure she could keep a secret because she was always known for running back telling Cheryl things that I shared with her, so I thought because she always found out stuff I was doing.

"So, what are you going to do, because you do know that is the first question Cheryl is going to ask you when you tell her." She said as she was shaking her head.

"I am not sure, yet. That's why I have not told anyone else. Only you and DBoy know about it, and you know he is unhappy about it." I told her. She already knew how he felt about me getting pregnant from previous conversations me and her had about it.

"Well, just be prepared to raise this baby on your own just in case he decides to leave you." She said telling me something I already knew. I always said if I was to ever have a baby, I would give it the world because growing up the way I did was rough as fuck and it fucked me up. As bad I tried to break generational curse, it was bad for me. The only generational curse I broke was using drugs. Yeah, I smoked weed but I was not robbing, stealing, and killing looking for my next high. We went into the house and celebrated Mother's Day. After dinner and exchanging gifts, I went home to lay down. I was tired and full of all the food that was over there.

I had not talked to DBoy all day, so I called him myself. I guess he was about to start being an extra asshole towards me because he could tell I wanted to keep the baby.

"Hello?" He answered all dry.

"Damn, I have not talked to you all day. What's up?" I asked him.

"Nothing, chilling, watching TV. What's up Rochelle?" He asked still dry.

"Can I come see you?" I felt like I was kissing his ass, but I needed to know where his mind frame was at. I knew his favorite saying was get pregnant and I am going home but I knew deep down in my heart that nigga loves me, and he is not going nowhere.

"Yeah, Rochelle." Still dry, but I did not care. I was still on my way to him. When I arrived at his mama's house as always, I went right to him and sat on his futon. The only thing he said to me was, "Can you make some lasagna for me?" Of course, I said yes and went to the kitchen to get it done. His vibe was way off and different and I could feel it.

After dinner, I took my clothes off to take shower. As I did, he looked at me and said, "Your stomach is big as fuck now that I look it. Your ass been pregnant."

"Well, I just ate too Bryce and I don't know how far I am. So, what are your thoughts on this? Touch it." I looked at him, unsure what he was going to say but prepared to get my feelings hurt.

"I'm not touching it. If you just have an abortion, we can just move out of town and get married after I get this case over with." He said bribing me to get the abortion in return for something I always wanted, just to be me and him.

"It is fucked up that I have to choose but I knew that was some weak ass shit you would do." I replied with tears in my eyes.

"You been knowing since day one I did not want no more kids right now." He said to me reminding me of his saying.

After that conversation, I was just ready to go to sleep. I passed out and he did not wrap his arms around me not one time. The next few days were the hardest for me. DBoy was ignoring my calls and giving me the smallest amount of attention. It was many days I laid in the bed crying, hurt and confused as to what I just got into. I was confused on if I choose the man I love or the baby I was carrying. At this point,

DBoy told me I could not come to spend the night over his mama's house, and he would see me on his passes out. I was still his runner, and that was the most conversation I got from him.

I finally got the balls to call and let Cheryl know that I was pregnant, and like everyone else who knew DBoy, I knew the reply would be negative.

"Hey ma, I have some news to call and let you know." I said scared as to what her reply was going to be.

"Um, okay, this does not sound good." She replied.

"I am pregnant." I said fast and ready for her reply.

"O, wow. So, what do you plan to do?" I knew that was going to be her first question.

"I really do not know at this point, which is why I am just now telling you. DBoy does not want the baby of course and I am just stuck between choosing him or my unborn child. I am so stressed out, I have been crying for days. I am so lost and confused, ma." I started balling over the phone.

"Well, keeping a baby is not going to keep a man. You must be prepared to be a single mother if you do have this baby. He told you that he did not want any more kids. You do not need kids right now. You need to really take this into consideration. Abortion may be the best thing for you right now." She told me, which was what I knew she would suggest.

"Ugh, I just need time to think about all of this. It is just so much to take in." I replied. After our goodbyes, we hung up the phone. I knew it would be something I needed to figure out and I needed to do it fast because if I was getting an abortion, I needed to do it sooner than later.

Chapter 17
Choose Wisely

Never in a million years could I have imagined that I would be placed in such a situation where it came down to choosing my man over my unborn. Many of you may view me as weak minded but abuse measured in mind control is a motherfucker.

Now, I was having morning sickness every day. I felt like shit. I finally decided to set my appointment for my abortion which the first appointment was set for the following day. It was not what I wanted to do but DBoy and Cheryl talked me into doing so. DBoy would not let me come over his mama's house because he did not want anyone to know I was pregnant, and the way the morning sickness was set up, I would give it all away, and the little bump I had would tell it all too.

Since my abortion appointment was set, DBoy was being a little nice to me. He had a run I needed to make for him, so I had to go get the cocaine from his house. Shortly after I sat on the couch, his other baby mama came walking through the door with a huge belly bump. She came for some money and as she stood there, he thought it was okay to let me know something.

"That is my baby in there." She just stood there smiling. She did not say if it was or was not. After she left, he continued to tell me that was his baby. Finally, after I got in my feelings, he told me he was just playing. Hell, at this point I did not know what to believe.

The next morning arrived and I had no strength or energy to make it to this first appointment for the abortion. However, I knew it was something I needed to do. As soon as I rolled over, I threw up all over the place. I did not know if this was normal or if it was just stress. Finally, up and dressed, I left the house. I did not have anyone to go with me, so I went alone. As I pulled in, it was protestors standing outside the building with signs. The shit made me sick to my stomach. I got there and checked in. As I sat in the waiting room, my leg would not stop shaking from my nerves. I looked around the waiting room to see if anyone knew me, but this was something I had to keep a secret.

"Rochelle," the nurse called me. My stomach started to turn as I walked to the back. The lady took me to a room with a TV.

"This is a two-appointment procedure. This first appointment you will watch a video of our two abortion options, which are either a pill and you pass at home, or you can have the procedure. After you watch the video, you will have an ultrasound, which...."

She was still going on, but I stopped her before she could finish.

"Do I have to have an ultrasound?" I asked not wanting to hear the baby's heartbeat nor see it.

"Yes, you must, that is not a choice. After that, we will have some paperwork for you, determine your due date and we will set up your procedure date. Do you have any more questions?" The lady asked me.

"No!" I replied as a tear fell down my face. She put the video on and walked out of the room leaving me alone. Halfway through the video I had a breakdown, crying so hard and yelling.

"Why me?" The nurses came running in the room to check on me.

"Are you okay?" The nurse asked as she squatted down to be eye to eye level with me.

"Um, no I am not. I can't do this. I have to leave this place." I said crying and gasping for air.

"Okay, you can leave, but I need you to calm down and relax first. Sydney go get her some water and napkins, please?" She told the other nurse who came to check on me as well once they heard my screams. As I calmed down and caught my breath, I took a sip of the water and wiped my face. "Thank you ladies so much. I am going to go. I need more time to think this over." I left the building, got in my car and had no plans to look back. I knew calling DBoy or Cheryl to let them know I just could not bring myself to do that was out. The thought of not having anyone during this time hurt me a lot, and once again the tears came rolling down my face. As I drove past the protestors, a sign caught my eye.

ABORTION IS MURDER! I did not want to be a murderer, I wanted to be a mommy.

Modeling was still a big dream that I had, which I was holding on to regardless of the fact I was carrying life inside of me and had a baby bump. My agent set me with a fashion show but because of my stomach showing I had to wear a dress. To my surprise, I asked DBoy to come support me. I was not sure if he would or not. Once it was my time to rip the runway, the first person I set my eyes on was him, DBoy. As I walked down the runway with my belly showing and my cute runway walk the MC was describing my dress.

"Our next model is Rochelle, who is wearing our long elegant silk dress. As you all can tell she is with child, so our dresses are fit for all." As she said that, I rubbed my belly, looking over at DBoy to see his reaction but still smiling to the audience. He kind of rolled his eyes and shook his head. During the intermission from the show, they served us food. As I was sitting next to DBoy, many people gave me compliments and congratulated me on the life I was carrying. DBoy hated it. Every time someone said something about the baby, he would turn his head, not paying the situation too much mind. After one compliment, he looked at me.

"I'm still not happy and you look ugly." That was the least of the mean shit he said to me so I did not get in my feelings. I just rolled my eyes at him and went back to my plate. I had my face beat, hair done, and I was glowing as everyone was saying. I finally felt good about myself, and here I had him in my ear telling me I was still ugly. The mental abuse started happening a little too often, but I was finally getting to the point that his words were not hurting me. At least I tried not to let them.

After the fashion show, we went to DBoy's mother's house for a family barbeque. He had a messy ass auntie who they called Aunt Jean. She was an old messy lady. I could not stand her. When we arrived, she was the first person who saw me. Running towards us being her messy self she yelled.

"Ummmm, what is that bump in your shit?"

Playing it off like I had no idea what she was talking about

"What bump? You are seeing stuff. How have you been Aunt Jean?" I was acting like I cared to take the attention off me.

"I been good girl, you know me. Just working, but I am trying to figure out what you have going on here." She asked still wanting to know my business.

"Aunt Jean, go on now. Ain't nothing going on." DBoy jumped in to cut me off from saying anything else and getting irritated once again like he always did when it came to this life I was carrying that he did not want.

After his family barbeque and everyone was gone, I decided it was time for me to tell DBoy what happened at Planned Parenthood. I let him know I decided to keep the baby. It was a conversation I was not ready to have but I know it was needed.

"Well Bryce, I guess it is no better time to talk than now. No point in drawing this whole process out. I am keeping my baby." I told him, waiting for a reply.

"Yep and you know I do not want no more kids. So what?" he said waiting on my reply.

"Welp, I will get with you in a few days and let you know what I come up with." I replied.

I left his mama's house in tears of course. I was hurt but I was sure I was making the right decision. I did not want to keep that house because of all the memories plus all DBoy's bitches knew where that house was. As bad I did not want to, I thought about staying with Cheryl because I did not have nowhere else to stay. I wasn't about to stay at that house dealing with DBoy and his disrespectful ways, so I had to do what I had to.

"Ma, hey. You busy? I need to talk to you." I said worried of her reply.

"No Rochelle, what is going on?" She replied.

"Okay, well last week I went to Planned Parenthood for my abortion appointment and I was not able to go through with the procedure. DBoy does not want much dealings with us. I told him he can have the house and I will leave, but I don't have nowhere to go. Can I come and stay with you until I get on my feet?" I took a deep breath waiting on her reply.

"Well, you know I already have a full house with Justin and his kids. I must let him know what is going on. When do you plan on moving in?" she asked.

"ASAP, I am just trying to find somewhere to lay my head right now so I can be done with DBoy, he can have the house." I told her as a tear fell down my face. I have always been a crybaby, whether it's a happy or sad situation. I had to swallow my pride and let DBoy know he could have the house and I was moving out.

"Yeah, Rochelle." He answered once again dry as hell.

"You can have the house, I will be moving out. I just ask that you take care of the shit because it is in my name." I told him, not giving too much detail on where I was going to see if he cared enough to ask, and of course he did not.

"Yep, just let me know when you are moved out. Are you taking the furniture with you?" He asked of course worried about himself.

"No Bryce, you can have all that shit there, even the fucking dog." I got an attitude fast at how selfish he was being. He was being an asshole and being mean to me like I got myself pregnant. I hung up on him before he had the chance to say anything. I never cried as much as I have the past few weeks since I found out I was pregnant; this was supposed to be one of the happiest moments in my life.

Last time I asked DBoy if he had Sickle Cell trait, he wouldn't tell me a flat-out answer. All he would say is "Just be ready to take care of a sick baby." I have the sickle trait so if I have a baby with someone who has a trait, then my baby would have Sickle Cell disease. He played mind games, so I just let it go over my head. That was Cheryl's argument to when trying to convince me to have an abortion. I still had it set in my mind that I was ready to be a mommy, sick baby and all. I was still going to do what I had to do for me and my baby.

I was finally settled in Cheryl's house, even though it was 6 people: me, her, her boyfriend and his 3 kids. I must say she did make sure that I was comfortable. I slept in his daughter's bed and she slept on the couch. Morning sickness was an everyday, all day thing for me. It was rough as hell. Cheryl got me some peppermints to suck on every morning as soon as I woke up. Some days it worked and other days it didn't. I had my first doctor's appointment and they gave me a due date of January 5. Me and Patricia started becoming close again now that she knew me and DBoy was not fucking around no more. We talked daily on the phone.

Even though me and DBoy were not together, he still called me to make his runs. As normal, he called me and told me to go to the house, get a pound of weed and take it to his Pops' house. It was 9:30 PM and even though I was in bed, I got up to do what he wanted me to do as always.

Chapter 18
Emotions

With no questions asked, I was headed out west to the house to make this run for him. I pulled up and he ran out with the weed wrapped up in a hoodie. The way he ran out was a little bit suspicious, like he had a bitch in there, but my pregnant ass had no energy to even say anything. I took my normal route to his Pops' house. I noticed a car was following me from the busy street by our house for about 10 minutes. After I got over the bridge, I'll be damned if it was sirens pulling me over. I slowed down and was shaking. The weed was rolled up in the hoodie in the front seat. I started to toss it to the back seat, but they ran up on me so fast I had no time. As I pulled over, I saw 3 more police cars line up in a row. As they jumped out, the first one was holding his gun pointing at me and yelling.

"Put your hands out the window." Shaking, I did as I was told. I had no idea what was going on as he walked up to my window I asked.

"Sir, what did I do?" My belly was big so he could see I was pregnant.

"Your car matches the description of a car that was involved in a robbery, but it's evident you are not the person so enjoy your night." He said as he flashed his flashlight in my truck. Other cops walked up with their guns drawn and flashlights out. I hoped and prayed they did not smell the fresh pound of weed I had sitting in the seat.

"Thank you, sir." Still shook up, I put my truck in drive and pulled off. As soon as I pulled off, I called DBoy to let him know what happened.

"I was just pulled over by four cop cars. They had me put my hands out the truck window saying my truck matched the description of a truck that was just involved in a robbery and flashing the flashlight all in my truck." I told him panicking still.

"Man, what the fuck? Did they let you go?" He asked quickly.

"Yeah they did, I am gone now headed to your Pops' house. I am nervous. That shit was strange to me." I told him, damn near ready to turn the truck around and take that shit back to DBoy's house.

"Awe okay. You good just drop that shit off at Pops' and head home." He told me, which I figured he would because he was all about his money. I finally got to his pops, dropped the pound of weed off, took the money to the house and headed to Cheryl's house. DBoy kept all his shit at the house I gave him, so it was still close and easy access for him.

As soon as I got to the house, I showered and laid down. It was about 12:30 am when I finally laid down and my phone started ringing. As I looked at the caller ID on my phone, it said "Unknown". I had no idea who could be possibly be calling my phone this late and private at that.

"Hello." I answered sounding like I was half asleep.

"I am trying to confirm that you are pregnant by Bryce?" The hoe said snappy.

"Who the fuck is this?" I snapped back.

"This is Shae, and I need to know are you pregnant by him?" She answered, like it was okay to be calling my phone.

"Bitch, get you some business." I told her as I hung up the phone. The bitch blew my phone up for about 30 minutes until I finally turned my phone off.

The next morning, the first thing I did was call DBoy to tell him about his messy ass baby mama, Shae. He replied.

"Yeah, Aunt Jean went running her mouth to her. Just ignore the shit." That was his favorite line to say when me and her had a run in. The bitch knew I was pregnant, so what the fuck was the point in calling me? To be messy. I got up and got dressed for work. Working and sitting all day at work was starting to take a toll on my feet causing them to swell bad. It was something that I had to do, especially now that I was about to be a mommy.

Warning Before Destruction

Going to my doctor appointments and taking my prenatal as well as Folic Acid became the normal for me. On top of morning sickness every day, my face was breaking out bad. My nose was so big and swollen. I was so big, people would always tell me it was more than one baby, but I knew it was just one. I was eating everything you could think of. It was from depression. I could not do nothing else to cope with the daily stress of life but eat. DBoy never touched my belly, he hated me. This pregnancy was so hard for me, and I felt so alone. Cheryl did not touch my belly either. When I was having a pain, she would just talk.

"You are pregnant, Rochelle."

She had a few miscarriages with her current boyfriend, so that may have something to do with it, but she never really stated if that was the case. If you don't tell me the answer, then the answer I made up in my head was right. I just thought she did not want to be bothered with me and my unborn child. My belly was poking out and I wanted to hurry up and take maternity pictures before the winter came. I did not feel cute, but I still wanted to take them as a memory of my first love.

The pictures were set for the next day and I did not have nothing to wear so I called DBoy and told him I needed some money. After he continued to play me about the money, I decided to pull up to the house because I knew he was out on a pass and more than likely that's where he was chilling.

Homer's was no longer the spot, it was too risky partying without legal coverage needed to run an under 21 club. I pulled up and honked the horn as well as called him to let him know I was there. He looked out the window and ran out to my truck. Grabbing his meat roll out his pocket he knew I was pulling up for some money. As he was counting out the money, I looked at the house and seen a female walk by in some booty shorts and a tank top.

"I have to pee." I told him as I was opening the door, just so I could be nosey and see who was in the house that was still in my name.

"Nah man. Here go this money. Now you need to get from around here." He said as he was pushing my door shut. I had a belly but that was not my thought at that time. As always, my emotions got the best of me, and I reacted.

"No, let me pee and then I will leave." I said pushing on the door.

"Alright Rochelle. Go pee and then you have to get the fuck out." He yelled as he followed me in the house. As we were walking toward the house, the bitch walked back past the door the opposite way. I got to the door and walked in. I went to the bathroom, while he went to the living room. After I used it and washed my hands, I walked to the kitchen and politely asked questions to the bitch who was doing dishes.

"And who are you?" Before I could get closer to the girl, DBoy had swooped me up and carried me out the front door. On the porch, he put me down on my feet. I looked down and seen a glass with ice water in it. I bent over to pick the glass up so I could launch it at him. While my hand was on top of the glass ready to pick it up, DBoy stomped on my hand with all his might, causing the glass the break in my hand. As I stood up, yelling and looking at my hand it was dripping blood like a water faucet.

"You stupid bitch. You see what you did to me?" I lifted my hand up and blood flung on him.

"Man, you are dumb as fuck. Get the fuck away from here. Now, get in your truck and leave. I am calling your mom to come get your retarded ass man. I cannot believe you came over here on that shit." He was yelling as I was standing there with a face full of tears. He started reaching for his phone to call Cheryl. The bitch stayed in the house the whole time which if she knew what was best for her, she did the right thing. I was in monster mode, pregnant and all. I would have ripped her head off her shoulders. I knew me and DBoy was not together but the fact he had another bitch already killed me and hurt my feelings. She looked young, she was a little cutie with a nice shape. He finally got Cheryl on the phone while I was sitting on the porch refusing to leave while my hand leaked.

Warning Before Destruction

"ROCHELLE! Get your ass in that truck and leave now before someone calls the police on you, out here acting a damn fool and you're pregnant." Cheryl rarely cussed but the way she just cussed me out, I knew she was not playing. I was living under her roof at this time, so I did as she told me to do and leave. I did not say one word, just cried from the pain in my hand, and the pain from such a bad heartbreak. I felt like shit. Everything was so fucked up, and this was supposed to be the time I was glowing and happy. This bitch ass nigga was making my life a living hell.

I got in my truck and went up the street to St. Vincent Hospital Emergency Room. My hand was still leaking, and when I pushed on it, I could feel the glass in it. I went to the emergency room alone and did not call nobody. Cheryl was blowing my phone up, but I did not want to hear her mouth. Once I got back to the room, I got a Tetanus shot. They cleaned the cut, pulled the glass out and stitched my hand up. I had to lie about how it happened so they would not get the police or CPS involved since I was acting crazy while with child. In the hospital room waiting on my discharge papers, I held my belly and rubbed it, while talking to my unborn baby. I was telling it how sorry I was and how I am going to do better for its sake, as well as mine. I knew how it felt to grow up with no mother and that was a pain I did not want my baby to experience so I had to get it together. I finally got my discharge papers and was headed to Cheryl's house. It was late, and everyone was asleep. I quietly hopped in the shower and laid down. My pregnant body was so exhausted that I immediately passed out.

I had so much going on that I forgot about the apartment that I gave to DBoy's brother until I got a call from the leasing office saying it was an unpaid balance that needed to be paid. He left the apartment a month before the lease was up and did not pay the last month. He left a lot of damages too, I was pissed. No point in calling DBoy, he was just going to be an asshole like always. Seems like every time I did something nice for somebody, the shit would backfire on me. I did not have plans to live with Cheryl for too long, so I had to get that shit paid off. I went to the apartments and set up payment arrangements.

With stitches in my hand, the next day arrived and it was time for my maternity photos. I hid them the best I could, so they would not show in my pictures and plus I did not want my model agent to ask me no questions about what happened. The shoot was good. My agency did my make up, so I was feeling a little pretty. That was a very happy moment in my life, and I was not going to let anything ruin it.

Chapter 19
The Big Set Up

Shit between me and DBoy was a love hate thing. We would not discuss the baby at all. We were only having conversations because I was still his runner. I was sure once he was off house arrest, he would probably cut me off from that too. We were not having sex, no hugging, no kissing, no I love you, nothing. He would only call when he wanted something, or he needed me to make a run for him. I was not getting no affection from no one while I was pregnant with DBoy's child. He would still bad mouth me and make jokes.

"Whose baby is that? The mailman's?" However, I was still in my feelings about him. I wanted to be a family with me, him and our baby. He did not want to, and I could not make him, or do anything to change his mind.

Like always, he called me to make a run for him. He had me meet him at his pops' house. He had a bitch name Nicole. They had been fucking around for years. They did not have any kids together but DBoy took care of her kids like they were his own. Her son's father had got killed in front of him when he was young, so DBoy decided to step up and be a father figure. She did his hair and every time he went, I would get shitty. Even though they were not together, she was cool with him fucking around, if he fucked her too. She was another one who was moving his work throughout the city. As I pulled up to his pops' house, I did not call. I got out and walked to the back where everybody was hanging out. When I walked around the house to the back, I seen DBoy sitting in a chair and Nicole sitting on his lap. He tried to be funny and introduce us.

"Rochelle, this Nicole." He said as he as he pointed to us each.

"Hey girl. How are you?" She said to me with a big smile on her face as she got up off him. I looked at her, rolled my eyes and took a seat in the chair next to him. I could tell I ruined the conversation. A few seconds after I sat down, she left walking to the front of the house. He was talking to all his family and friends as if I was not there. His phone was sitting in his lap face up. A text message from Nicole showed up saying Can I have you tonight daddy?

As I always did, I reacted off emotion. I snatched his phone off his lap before he could grab it and ran to my car. I locked my doors immediately so he could not get to me. I had my car pulled up in the driveway right behind his car so he could not move until I moved my car. I kept a knife in my car because if I ever ran into Shae again, I was going to kill her. I pulled the knife out because as soon as he went to the back of the house, I was going to flatten his tires. Nicole's bitch ass was standing on the front porch the whole time. I could have beat her ass too, but I stayed in my truck.

"Move you bumpy face ass bitch." He yelled knowing how sensitive I was about my face as it was breaking out. I would not move my car to let him get out, so he hopped in his truck, started it up, and rammed backwards into my truck, causing his back bumper to come off. He hopped back out his truck and picked up a huge brick. He lifted it above his head yelling.

"I am about to throw this brick if you don't move your muthafucking truck, Rochelle. Damn man, I hate you bitch." I knew he was crazy enough to throw the brick, so I put my truck in reverse and backed out. Once I backed out, he jumped in his truck fast and pulled out. I was not done yet. I followed him and he took me on a high-speed chase. He was speeding thru alley's and on busy streets. I was on his ass the whole time. We finally arrived at our old house. DBoy pulled up in the driveway and got out. As he got out, I pulled up in the grass of the front yard trying to run him over with my truck. He finally got in the house and shut the door. My phone rang from a number which was not saved in my phone. I picked up.

"Aye bitch, you better leave my fucking baby daddy alone and go find the daddy of that baby. You keep playing with his freedom and tearing up his shit, taking from his kid's mouths. If I must beat your ass, then I will. Leave him the fuck alone you young...." She hollered, and I hung up before she could finish. It was Tosha. That threw me over the edge. I hopped my pregnant ass out the car, went to his truck and started kicking the shit out of it with all the strength I had. DBoy came running out of the house as he saw me kicking his shit. It was a huge dent in the door. I was too big to run and get in my truck before he caught me. He ran up behind me putting his hands around my neck. All I could do was think about my baby when he choked me, scared he would cut the baby's circulation off too, He had his hands around my neck long enough to tell me get away.

"I don't know why you keep fucking playing with me, man. Get in your fucking truck and leave man. Damn." He let my neck go and I ran to my truck. As I got in my truck, he went back into the house. I was sitting in the truck balling my eyes out with my truck still in the middle of the front yard. The two police cars pulled up blocking me in. My heart dropped, and I started to feel a sharp pain in my stomach. The officers got out the car and came to my window.

"What is going on, ma'am? Why is your truck in the middle of the yard like this?" He asked me.

"I just need to go home, sir. Please just let me go home." I cried, and not wanting to tell on myself so I avoided their questions. The other officer walked off going to the door to speak to DBoy. One of the neighbors must have called the police because I knew for a fact DBoy didn't. After the officer talked to DBoy, he came and told me that I needed to leave the premises and not return, or I was going to jail. They moved their cars and I pulled out the yard. I still was not done with him. I was so full of hurt and bitterness that I needed to get him somehow. I went to the gas station around the corner for a minute to give them time to leave. While at the gas station, I cleaned my face off. I had scratches all on my chest and neck from wrestling with him. On my way back around the corner, my phone rang again from Tosha's number.

"What, bitch." I snapped as soon as I answered.

"Let me see you before you have that baby, and I promise you won't have it." She threatened me and my unborn.

"You are calling me concerned about OUR baby daddy, but you need to focus on buying your son some clothes that fit and get his haircut." I snapped on her. She always sent her son to my house with too big clothes and his hair not cut.

"Bitch, now I am out to find you. You done took shit too far talking about my son. That's why your nasty ass don't know who your baby daddy is." That must have been some bullshit DBoy told her. I knew who my baby daddy was, and I would prove to her as soon as my baby is born it is his.

"Bitch, your son calls me mama." I said laughing and hung up the phone in her face.

Warning Before Destruction

As I pulled back on the street, I could still see the police in front of the house. I turned my truck around and called Patricia. I wanted to flatten his tires but the way my fat ass was set up, I could not bust them and run to the car. When I called Patricia and explained the story to her, she was down and ready to ride. She was five minutes from the house. I picked her up and we went and scoped out the scene. The door was shut, and so was the blinds. The sun was going down, so it was not too bright outside. I parked on the corner while she ran a few houses down. She got the two passenger tires good and ran back to the car. I dropped her off and headed to the other side of town to Cheryl's house.

About 30 minutes later, DBoy started blowing my phone up. I knew it was just for him to cuss me out about his flat tires, so I did not answer. After many calls and no answer, he sent me a text

I better not ever see you again. I am going to fuck you up. You called my son dusty and you flattened my fucking tires.

Once again exhausted, mentally, physically and emotionally, I jumped right in the bed. My baby was not moving and had not been for a few hours. This was not the first episode where my baby was not moving. Last time I called the doctor, he told me to drink something cold and lay on my left side. I got up and drank some milk, went back to lay down and held my belly while once again apologizing to my unborn for all the stress I have been going through. The baby finally moved; my nerves were at ease. I turned my phone off and passed out.

I woke up the next morning sore as fuck from head to toe. Morning sickness was kicking my ass. I had FMLA, so my job was secured. Thank God for good benefits from my job. I had to call into work. I was so fucked up. I laid in the bed and had many thoughts going through my head. I had finally come to the reality that I needed to cut all ties with him, and that included telling him he had to get out of that house. My love for him had turned into hate. I hated everything about him. I was willing to risk my credit for my peace and to have a healthy baby. My baby had been having times where it wouldn't move, Cheryl always told me the baby feels everything I feel. It was time I let DBoy let go.

DBoy called my phone that evening. I answered with an attitude "Yeah?"

"Did you call the Humane Society on my dogs, Rochelle?" He asked me.

"Man, what the fuck are you talking about?" I asked him, lost as to why he asked me that.

"When I got out on my pass, I went to the house. It was a note on the door from them and they took my fucking Pitts from the backyard." He snapped, I was just as confused as he was.

"I did not call them people, Bryce. It could have been the neighbors, Hell, I don't know." I told him.

"I am shitty, but ummm, I need you to go to the house, grab that 8 ball and drop it off at Buck's house for me. I would do it, but I am out fishing. Dude is going to give you $3,500. Give Buck $1,500. It is over a few grams but use the weight bench and break the extra off. I got another run for that when you get done." He said to me talking somewhat in codes over the phone. I understood what he was saying. After getting the strength to get up and go across town, I pulled up to the house, got the key from under the rug, went to the drawer where he had the *hard* hidden at. I grabbed it and put it inside my purse, locked the door back and put his key back under the mat.

It has been awhile since I've seen Buck, not since I've been pregnant. I put his address in my GPS and headed to the house. When I pulled up, it was a white man standing on the porch with his hands in his pocket pacing back and forth. Before I went to the doorstep, I called DBoy.

"Yeah." He answered the phone.

"It is a white man standing on the porch at Buck's house. Is it still cool to go in?" I asked him, not having a good feeling about serving this man.

"Yeah, it's all good. Just handle it and call me when you're done." He answered me, sounding confident that shit was cool. He said shit was alright, so I hopped out and wobbled my fat ass across the street. As I walked up, he greeted me with his dark shades on.

"How are you?" He asked me as he followed me in the house.

"I am good. Thanks." I replied, as I walked in, I saw Buck standing there.

"Damn, you pregnant? It's been a while since I've seen you." Buck greeted me.

"Yeah, it's been awhile since I've seen you." I replied to him.

"The weight bench is on the table, DBoy said it was a little over." Buck said as he points to the scale on the table. The white man stood in the corner counting his money out. I could not tell if he was looking at me or not because his sunglasses were so dark. I wobbled around the table, I sat on the couch right in front of the scale and weighed out the correct amount for the man. I broke the little piece off and put it back in my purse. I bagged the big brick up, and I handed it to the white man.

"$3,500 right?"

"Yeah." I replied as we made the exchange. The white man stood there with this purchase in his hand and watched as I counted out $1,500 for Buck. I handed it to him and made my way out the door. As soon as I got in the car, I called DBoy.

"It's done, just send the address for the rest and I'll take your money to the house." I told him as soon as he answered the phone.

"It's BoxHead and them over there in HaughVille." He told me.

"Yep." And I hung up the phone.

I made the last run and took his money to the house like I told him I would. I had plans to call him later and tell him he needs to have all his shit out of the house. I made up my mind I was done and washing my hands with him. That was my last run I was making for him. I was going to meet him tomorrow to help him get his shit out, and I was getting a new phone number.

I finally made the call to him. I did not know how he was going to take it, but he was done with me so I figured he would make this process easy.

"Yeah," he answered like he always did.

"Tomorrow you need to be out of that house, I am giving it back to the people, that way we can be totally done with each other. I'll meet you there tomorrow when I get off work so I can get the key and turn it in to the leasing agent." I told him. It was a pause on the phone, "Um, hello?" I asked to make sure he was still on the line.

"You aint shit muthafucka." He said as he hung up the phone. I shot him a quick text saying,"

Just make sure you are out my shit tomorrow.

. He did not reply. I did not expect him to, but I was damn sure pulling up on him tomorrow when I got off work to make sure this shit got handled.

All day at work, DBoy had been calling my phone all day talking shit about me putting him out the house. That shit did not move me, at this point I just wanted to cut all ties with him.

Chapter 20
The Guts to Let it Go

After a long day of work, I was exhausted, but I still had to drive to the west side of town. As soon as I got off, that was my first stop. I had it set in my mind that fighting and arguing with him was not going to happen. That's when I knew I was done. I pulled up and he had a U-Haul in the front yard, I wobbled up to the front door.

"I am not here on no bullshit, I just needed to see how much you had done." I said to him in the calmest voice. He was cracking jokes and moving as slow as he could, he wanted a reaction from me so bad, but I refuse to give him that energy. In the bedroom, I pulled off the mattress pillow top to place it in a bag so I could take it with me. He walked up to me yelling.

"You ain't taking shit from here."

"Boy, you live with your fucking mama on a futon. Why do you need this?" I asked him, still calm.

He walked over to the dresser and grabbed the knife that was sitting there. He started stabbing the mattress top and tearing all the stuffing out.

"Because bitch, you want to put me out, you can't take shit from here that I paid for." I walked out the room, went to the bathroom to use it. I went back to the room. He was in the garage moving shit, and he still had all his clothes and shoes. As I bent down to pick up another handful of his shoes, he pushed me.

"Bitch don't touch my shit; I don't need your help."

"I am not giving you this energy; I am going to call the police." As I walked to the living room to call the police, he was still yelling. As soon as the police pulled up, so did his mom and Tosha. I remember the threat Tosha just made when me and DBoy was into it, and as bad as I wanted to tear her head off her shoulders, I knew I could not be fighting. When they pulled up, I went out to my truck and sat. As they were helping, I could hear them talking shit about me, but it did not move me. The police finally arrived. I did not tell them full details of what happened because I did not want to risk his freedom. The officer told him to move his things as fast as he could and told me to stay in my truck. After the police left, Tosha came to my window and started talking her same bullshit about how I was a whore and needed to find my baby daddy. I was proud of myself for not acting a plum ass like I would have. While he was moving out, he told me his Pitt Bulls got a hold of Tyson and broke his neck and killed him. After an hour of waiting, he was finally all moved out.

On the way home to Cheryl's house on the other side of town, I called the cell phone company to get a new phone number. It was time for change, and I had full control. Cutting him off was hard to do. The thought of raising my child without a father also hurt me, but it was something I was prepared to do.

It had been a few weeks since I talked to DBoy, but I must say it has also been the most peaceful few weeks I've had since I've been pregnant. I finally found out I was giving life to a baby boy. Morning sickness was still kicking my ass. They offered me medication, but I was worried about taking anything other than my prenatal and Folic Acid pills. I was carrying a whole lot of water; everything was swollen from my nose to hands down to my feet. I was carrying so much extra weight everyone thought I was further along or having twins. I was told by a coworker, who I bonded with, to watch myself because I could be getting preeclampsia. I told my doctors, but they said if my blood pressure was not high then I was okay.

Every morning like always, I took Cheryl's boyfriend's kids to school. This morning was nothing new until I got up out of bed to a sharp pain. When I got to the toilet, the pain became more and more sharp. The pain was so unbearable I had to sit on the toilet with a pillow on my belly. The kids began to panic as I screamed and cried for God to please take the pain away. They called Cheryl who to my surprise immediately left work and came home. I finally calmed down and was headed to the emergency room. I thought I was losing my baby. Cheryl had to go back to work, so like always I was on my own. As I sat in the room waiting for the doctor to come back, I had another breakdown, crying and holding my stomach, letting my baby boy know I was sorry for my actions and we are going to be alright. The doctor came in and told me I was dehydrated which was causing me to have contractions. After I got an IV, I was released. Like any other situation, I had to hear Cheryl's mouth about how I needed to focus on my health because I was carrying another life that I needed to focus on the birth of a healthy baby.

Me, Cheleste and Stephanie were back cool. Antwan was involved in a bad ass car accident. They called me and I was right there by his side. He had run his truck into a light pole and was in the ICU for a few days. Every day I made sure I went to visit him. We even discussed us getting back together. I was happy to have my besties back. It was often I drifted off as a loner or I did something to them, and we fell out. They were like family, and I knew when I needed to vent, they would be there for me like always. I was a hard pill to swallow, from my past and all the bullshit I endured during my life. I just had a zero tolerance for bullshit. My besties did not understand me, which I guess is why I was always the outsider. I was holding in so much bitterness and hate in me for everybody. I thought about therapy but that thought quickly changed to fuck it. This open case was stressing me out so much I even had thoughts of suicide.

Chapter 21
Plot to Kill Us

October 17 was a normal morning for me. I woke up, had my morning sickness episode, got dressed, dropped the kids off to school and was headed to work. I had a beauty shop appointment last night so I woke up with a little bit of confidence in myself. I was six months pregnant and my feet were so swollen, I could not wear shoes. I had to wear house shoes EVERYDAY. They were so swollen at times it hurt to even walk. It had been two months since I last spoke to DBoy, even though it hurt, I was getting used to doing things on my own.

I parked in my normal spot at work and wobbled into the building. I worked on the second floor, the steps were not an option for me. As I got off the elevators, I was greeted by my supervisor whose face was red and I could tell she had been crying.

"Good morning, Rochelle. I need you to come with me to the conference room, Someone is here and would like to meet with you." She said as she wiped her face. I was very confused as to what was going on, my first thought, I was about to get fired for my attendance, but other than that I didn't have the slightest idea who was coming to see me at my workplace.

As I walked into the conference room behind her, I saw two white men sitting at the table with a laptop set up. The white men were in street clothes, but as soon as I stepped in the room one approached me.

"I am Adam from the FBI Agency, and you are under federal surveillance at this time. The father of your child will never see daylight again." As he held his badge up for me to see it. My stomach dropped as I cried and began to scream.

"No, what the fuck is going on? I need answers." I yelled as I bent over trying to calm myself down.

"Calm down Rochelle, you have to breathe." My supervisor said as she rubbed my back to help me relax.

"Rochelle, we need you to calm down and have a seat so we can let you know what is going on, we don't want you to have this baby on us, please calm down." The FBI agent said to me. I calmed down but the tears would not stop falling, they instructed me to sit in front of the laptop, but they never told me what I did wrong for me to be in federal custody.

"We have a recording we need you to listen too, we cannot tell you the details of the case, but you are charged with conspiracy and four counts of dealing as of right now. This is a recording we have from a tracking device." I was confused as fuck, but I sat there and listened to the recording, it was a male voice having a conversation with another male.

"Yeah, cousin you can put some rat poison in her food, and it will kill the baby." The male said

"Alright, I am going to look into it because I cannot deal with that bitch and she refused the abortion as soon as I found out she was pregnant." The other male replied. It was a conversation between DBoy and his cousin. His cousin was telling him how he could kill my unborn son. Once again, I broke down hearing the man who I loved planning on killing my baby and possibly harming me. I could not understand for the life of me how DBoy could hate me so much. Yeah, I was pregnant, but I did not do it on my own, I mean this nigga sperm did meet... you get the point.

After I listened to the recording, the FBI Agent looked at me.

"It's clear Bryce does not care about you. On top of all the other girlfriends he has, this man is heartless." I did not reply, like DBoy always taught me, less is better.

"Okay so I need to know what is this all about? Where is he now?" I asked still crying, shook up and scared.

"Why would you want your son to be raised by such a monster? We are going to transport you to the federal building, the holding cell, where you will learn more about this case." The FBI Agent said to me as he was packing up his laptop.

"Can I call someone to come pick up my truck?" I asked worried about leaving my car parked at my job, I had no idea if they were going to let me go or if I was going to be stuck in jail. He gave me permission to call Cheryl. She was spazzing out over the phone asking me what happened.

"I don't know what is going on, Ma. I just need you to come and get my truck from my job. They are transporting me to the federal holding cell downtown where I have to talk to the detective. He said I am being charged with conspiracy to deal and two counts of dealing. I have to go now; they won't let me talk much on the phone." I told her. She replied okay still in shock like me and hung up the phone. Every time I got into some shit; Cheryl was the first person I would call.

As we exited the conference room from my job, the FBI Agent looked at me and said, "I will not put handcuffs on you, but I will walk close behind you." I guess they had some type of sympathy for my six-month pregnant, fat ass. On the 35-minute ride to the holding cell my thoughts were going nonstop. The main thought that bothered me was having my baby in prison and my son never being able to see his father. Like always when shit got real and I was a ball of emotions. My belly was too. I held my belly tight and told my son how sorry I was. When he put me in the car, he was talking to the other agent

"Okay, we have to go get the last one." I did not know who the last one was, so my mind started going crazy with thoughts. Right when I decided to get my life together and leave this fuck nigga alone, here it was. I was knocked back.

When we arrived at the federal holding cell underground, my stomach started to feel crazy. Right after I stepped foot out the detective's car, I threw up. My nerves were all fucked up. I had no clue what was about to happen to my freedom. I had no idea what I did wrong to be in this predicament. Even though it was many times I should have been locked up, and I didn't even have a juvenile record.

I was able to go to the bathroom to clean myself off. They took me to a room with no walls or windows, just a desk and chair.

"I am Detective Brad, the head detective in this case in this indictment. This is Jenny, the U.S. attorney Marshall. What details can you give us about the transaction that took place on July 29th at Bucks house?" As soon as I sat down, they got right to business. I remember this day, but I did not want to tell too much on myself.

"I do not want to speak until I get a lawyer." I said still crying and upset.

"Okay, we can lock you up right now, or you can tell us what you know." He started to get upset as the white lady wrote down notes.

"I dropped a package off to his house, that is all sir." I said trying to give less as I could.

"Did you know that package was crack cocaine." He asked.

"No sir." I played dumb.

"Was it in a clear baggie?" he asked, He knew what the fuck was going on.

"Yes." Caught up in my lie.

"So, what did you do with the rest of the grams?" He asked

"I went home with it, sir." I lied. The man and woman walked out the room for a minute, and came back in. The detective went right back to it. One thing about the feds, they don't come to pick you up until they have a solid case against you.

"I am going to ask you again, Ms. Brown." They knew I was lying.

"I told you, sir." I said sticking to my story.

"Well you sold to an undercover cop. We know what happened, but since you are not telling the truth, I will just take you to the holding cell." He was frustrated with me.

When I got to the holding cell, I walked past three cells before they put me in one. In the cell next to me was DBoy, and one of his close niggas.

"Damn, they done got my baby mama." DBoy said as I walked past him. They put me in the cell and shut the gate.

"You cool, baby mama?" he asked me through the bars. Now I was baby mama but the past few months he hasn't made no effort to check on me.

"Yep." I replied dryly, hoping he could sense my attitude.

"Welp, they kicked my mama's door down this morning, even had grandmama on the floor. They got both the safes, and they picked up six of us." He was telling me the scoop.

"Who were the six people?" I asked.

"Me, you, Trick, Buck, DJ, and Nicole." He said. I knew him and Nicole was fucking around, no other reason she was involved if they weren't.

"Um, well yeah I heard you plotting to kill my son with rat poisoning." I told him, letting him know I heard that shit.

"Man, they played that bullshit to get you to turn on me, and that was because the girl told me you gave her that morning after pill with your slick ass." He said, trying to make shit sound good. Him knowing I gave her the pill explained where all the stories about me trapping him came from. "So, it's a boy?" he continued to ask questions.

"Yep, my son." I told him.

"Damn, this shit is crazy. You know the motto, you don't know. Did they tell you what we're here for?" He was trying to whisper.

Warning Before Destruction

"Yeah, but you gotta take this man." I told him as a tear rolled down my eye, but I could not let him know I was crying so I quickly pulled myself together.

"Man come now BM, you know I can't take on shit extra." He said. If we were face to face, I would probably spit in his face for saying some dumb ass shit like that. I was done talking after that. He kept trying to make conversation and I kept ignoring him. They brought lunch finally and I was pissed. It was a soggy ass bologna sandwich, some soggy ass cookies, and a baby watered down lemonade. I yelled to the officer "I can't eat bologna." He did not give a fuck. He kept walking like he didn't hear me. The doctors told me when I eat lunch meat to heat it up in the microwave to kill the bacteria because it was harmful to the baby. After lunch, they came to get me and get my fingerprints, mugshot, sign paperwork and meet with the public defender, then placed me back in the cell. Finally, they came to get us for court. They chained us all together. As we got on the elevator DBoy touched my belly saying "Damn, I ain't going to see my son until he 18."

"Keep your hands to yourself," the guard said. Me and DBoy sat next to each other and his homeboy sat across from us, but Buck was nowhere to be found. As we walked into the courtroom, I seen Cheryl and mama Latifah sitting on the benches. It was a young bitch on the bench who kept making eye contact with DBoy, I guess that was his new bitch. They read the charges to us. The judge asked the prosecutor if I could be released.

"No priors, not a threat to society, and high-risk pregnancy, good job, and stable living with her mother. Yes, she can be released on pre-trial, as for Mr Bryce Gibson, he is being held with no bond at this time." It was like a weight lifted off me to know I was going to be released. As I walked out the judge said, "and you better be able to pass the drug test." Even though I took a few pulls from a blunt a few weeks ago, I knew I was cool.

I was released and Cheryl was there to pick me up. "I know this is a lot to process, so we will just discuss things later." As soon as we got to the house, Cheleste and Stephanie were already there to meet me and get the scoop on what just happened. We all just chilled and talked about what happened. They were so shitty I was in this situation. It was about to be a long drawn out process until I knew what my punishment was. My life was about to be placed on hold until then.

Chapter 22
Stress Can Kill

Cheryl and her boyfriend broke up, so we moved back home to Mama Latifah's house where we had to share a room. The next few weeks I did absolutely nothing but work and go home. I dealt with the stress of the case by overeating. My weight gain became so rapid and my blood pressure started to rise. I was high risk and had to go to doctor appointments weekly. Since I was not fully charged my job did not fire me yet, but I was so sick I started to miss too many days. I had FMLA so they could not fire me.

October 31, 2008, I was at work when I felt sharp pains in my belly. It felt like the pain I was feeling before when I was dehydrated. As the pain slowed down, I called my doctor's office and they told me to come in. Being that I was so high risk, every little ache and pain I was calling my doctor to make sure it was nothing to risk losing my baby. Stephanie came to get me from work and took me to my doctor's appointment. My blood pressure was 152/100, after a few blood pressure checks and having me lay on my side it would not go down. The doctor told me to go to the ER immediately. I called Cheryl on the way there so she could meet us. I was told I had preeclampsia and had to be admitted. My blood pressure was high, I had protein in my urine, abdominal pain, nausea and vomiting, and edema.

In the hospital, I was placed on bedrest for two weeks. My baby's due date was not until January, so they gave me a steroid shot to strengthen the baby's lungs. During those few weeks, most of the time I was alone. People came to check on my daily, but everyone still had their own lives to stick too. It was many times I cried and wondered how would shit have been if DBoy was home. We were not able to talk, so he would have random numbers calling me to check and see how shit was going. He still had no intentions on taking the full charges for the case. It was like every man for themselves.

The doctors told me there was no way to cure preeclampsia but to give birth. I was nowhere near dilated, my original due date was still two months away, and they did not want to put more stress on me and the baby by trying to make us go through labor.

After two weeks of bedrest in the Women's hospital, my doctor came in and told me "Tomorrow morning we are going to have an emergency C-section to deliver. Your condition is not getting any better and the baby is under too much stress right now." My 21st birthday I was going to be giving birth to my first born. Even though I was happy we would share the same birthday, I was scared because he was two months premature. The doctors told me for every month he was born early he would be one year behind, so my baby would be two years behind. I called Cheryl and told her the news. She came to spend the night with me so she could be in the surgery room with me the next day. She was all I had.

I was unable to sleep, my nerves had me up all night. 6:00 am arrived quick and it was time for me to get prepped for surgery. Cheryl got dressed in her surgery room gear. They placed my surgery IV in, shaved me up, wiped me down with some antibiotic soap, monitored me for a while and by 8:00 am I was being wheeled down to surgery to give birth to my son. I was scared from having a major surgery. All the risk they explained, and I did not know what was going to be the condition of my premature baby.

During the spinal tab I had to be alone, it was the worst pain. They had me sit on the edge of the surgery table, hunch my back out like cat, and stuck a long needle in my back which made me go numb, I was hollering at the top of my lungs. They brought in Cheryl as they started cutting me open.

"I heard you hollering, I didn't know what they were doing to you back here." She said jokingly. About 30 min into the procedure, I felt a push on my stomach, and I threw up as they pulled my itty-bitty baby out who was not making no noise. He was 3 pounds and 7 ounces, 19 inches long. After a few minutes, I looked at Cheryl and asked her "Why isn't he crying..." and before I could finish my sentence, I heard his little cries. The doctors rushed to get the baby plugged in to all the necessary cords and oxygen as well as placing him under the incubator light for warmth. They had to make like he was still inside the womb, warm and a good supply of food coming from me. After I was stitched back up it was time to go to the recovery room as they wheeled my baby away to the NICU. After 1 hour I was out of the recovery room and being wheeled in my hospital bed to the NICU to see my baby.

Still no name for my baby because DBoy wanted me to name him the 3rd child after him. My baby was so little. He was plugged up to so many cords and had a feeding tube going into his nose because the baby doesn't learn the sucking technique until they are 36 weeks in the womb. He was under a light that was keeping him warm. He had on a pamper and nothing else. As I touched his little foot through the hole in the incubator, I started to cry. Him was so little and a tiny part of me. This was someone who belonged to me and would never leave me. After a few minutes with the baby, it was time for me to head to my room. When I got to my room, it was Steven, Cheryl, Mama Latifah and a few of Cheryl's friends there, and so was DBoy's sister Ashley. They all made me feel loved, but the drugs were kicking in and I was in and out of sleep.

I was awaken by the nurse for a checkup. Everyone else was gone. In came the lactation nurse who brought me a pump and taught me how to pump, telling me that was the best thing

Warning Before Destruction

I could do for my son while he was sick. I began to pump like crazy, over the next few days. The nurses and doctor cleared me from labor. When it came time for my release, the nurses gave me the option to stay another night or to get discharged. I chose to stay another night with my baby.

The next day it was time for me to be released and I cried so hard. I had to leave my baby until he got strong enough to make it on his own which included him learning the sucking technique so he could eat on his own, gaining weight, being able to breathe on his own without the CPAP, and able to keep his body temperature at the correct rate degree of 99 Fahrenheit. I cried the first few days and had restless nights, from the pain of my C-section. I didn't have my own room. I had to sleep in the bed with Cheryl which was so uncomfortable. My adopted family, Cheryl's family was there for me during this time. Cheryl's brother Ejaz agreed to drive my car and take over my car note for me so I wouldn't be behind, and the doctors' orders was I could not drive until I was six weeks post-partum. Mama Latifah and Baba Musa would make sure I had a ride to and from the hospital every day, and mama Latifah even packed me a healthy lunch to nibble on while I spent all day, every day by my baby's side.

Everyday all day I went to sit with my baby in the NICU spending time with him as he was in an incubator. I pumped so much that my breast got engorged. I just wanted to give him all the nutrients he needed through my breast milk to make him strong and healthy. I decorated his area and even took him a few outfits. On the 5th day, I was finally able to hold my baby for the first time. His first holiday, which was Thanksgiving, he had to spend in the NICU, after going to Cheryl's family dinner I went to spend time with my baby. I brought my baby a *My First Thanksgiving* onesie and sweatpants to match. I made sure he was still dressed for the day He was making good and fast progress. Skin to skin, I would put him in my shirt. He was so small. The doctors told me skin to skin would keep him calm by laying his head on my heart and my body temperature would help his body temperature to stay regulated and at the rate it needed to be.

Meanwhile, my case was still in process. I was on pretrial, so I had to call a number every day to see if I had to take a drop. I had to deal with the people popping up and checking on me whenever they wanted to. To get a federal lawyer and for conspiracy it was racks that I did not have. DBoy made sure he had a paid lawyer though. The way he was playing like fuck me during this case was wild as fuck to me and making me hate him more and more.

Since I could not afford a lawyer, I had to get a public defender which I had to meet up with. She told me my charges hold between 5 and 10 years. I was scared. I had no idea what the hell I was going to do if I went to prison. She told me the

Warning Before Destruction

District Attorney wanted to have a meeting with me which she set up. During that meeting was more and more questions about what I knew about DBoy. They showed me pictures of guns, asked me about dead bodies, asked me about his dogs, asked about his baby mamas, and his kids. They told me they had been keeping close tabs on me. They explained how they knew about the police being called on me. They knew I got my number changed. They knew about everything that happened when I put DBoy out of the house. The feds had been watching us for months which is why I was pulled over when I was headed to his dad's house, and that explains who took his Pitts from the back. Court dates kept getting pushed back because they wanted to use me so bad to get on the stand and testify against him. That was something I did not want to do, and I knew it would be repercussions if I did. He would have me go over Nicole house to talk to him on her phone due to the judge placing a no contact order between me and DBoy. Soon, me and Nicole became cool and started to hang often.

Chapter 23
After the Pain

My baby boy was finally released from the NICU December 10, he was 1 month and 1 day old. It was one of the happiest days of my life, regardless of everything else going on. During the last month while he was in the NICU, I was getting everything set up and ready for him to come home. We got our own room in the house and no longer had to share with Cheryl. While on maternity leave even though I was living with Cheryl at her parents' house I still needed money. I was getting a partial check from my job, but I was also getting garnished from the house I let DBoy stay in. The few months he paid up in rent went by, so when I put him out rent was back to the monthly rate. I had to sign up for TANF, Medicaid, and CCDF. Ejaz taking over my car note for me was a huge blessing and help. If DBoy was out, I would not have to struggle the way I did. He was a womanizer, but he was always a great father to his kids.

I let Cheryl name my baby because she never had kids, so she picked him an African name to keep the culture of her family. Bryce wanted me to name my son after him, but I refused to. He did not deserve that privilege after how he neglected us my whole pregnancy and now ain't no telling how long he was going to be serving time and I was going to be out here raising my baby alone. I put a baby shower/naming ceremony together for my baby, that was African tradition to introducing a newborn to the world. My baby's name was Khari Gyasi which meant kingly and Gyasi meant power. It was a good turnout, even some of DBoy's family came. My baby got a lot of gifts and did not need or want for anything else.

DBoy would call my phone every blue moon when I had money on the phone. I made sure I sent him a lot of pictures of my baby though. This call he decided to inform me his cousin girl told him that I gave her the day after pill. The new story he had was I trapped him by not taking the morning after pill. It was time for me to go back to work, Cheleste grandma was an older lady who stayed at home, so she agreed to watch Khari every day for me for $50.00 a week which was something I could afford and I did not want him in a daycare with all those germs. He was premature so he had a weak immune system and could get sick fast.

All I did was work, take care of my son, stay at home, go to my court dates, and continue to do right on my pretrial. Shortly after I started to lose it and wanted to give up. Going back and forth to court and not knowing if I had to leave my unborn son, on top of losing my son's father to prison and being a full-time mother, it started taking a toll on me. I had an advantage of living with Cheryl because she was like an in-house babysitter, so it was easy for me to put Khari to sleep and run the streets. My baby boy has therapy sessions with a group called *First Steps.* Since he was premature and per studies for every month premature a child would be a month behind, he had to make sure he was up to speed. My baby was so up to date on all his skills that they decided to release him after his first initial sessions of therapy.

Me and Nicole started hanging together often. She started calling me "Baby Mama" and started calling Khari "Baby Bruh". It was her birthday and she wanted me to hang with her. I found me a cute outfit, got Khari settled for the night with Cheryl and was out in the streets. I was not a drinker or smoking. I couldn't do. We hit up the club and had a ball. I had a few drinks in me and was turned up. When we pulled back to her house to drop her off, we sat in the driveway and we talked.

"You ever fucked with a girl before?" She asked me as we sat in the truck.

"No, but I thought about it." I replied shyly.

"You want to try it for the first time?" She asked me.

"Yep." I said. I hadn't been touched in a long time out of respect for DBoy while I was pregnant. This was my first time, as nervous as I was, my little pussy was ready. As we walked in the house to her bedroom, we both took our clothes off and started sucking and rubbing all over each other. I laid her on the bed, and she opened her legs, as I went down and started giving her head. She moaned and said, "You sure this is your first time?"

I continued until she had an orgasm all over my face. She flipped me over and returned the favor. As I washed up, I got dressed and headed home to my baby boy. For the first time, I had my first sexual encounter with a girl, and it happened to be my baby daddy, baby mama.

The next day DBoy called and was making jokes about me and Nicole sleeping around. I didn't know if she told him or if he was just making jokes because he knew how freaky his BM was. I never told him yes or no, I just laughed and joked.

Over the next few months, I started to party and drink every off weekend I had a chance. Me and Nicole became running buddies, Cheryl did not trust her. Sometimes me, Cheleste, Stephanie and Patricia would all go out. When the FEDs raided Nicole's house, they found a gun in her kids play box. She was fighting a CPS case. My routine during the week was waking up, dropping Khari off at the babysitter, working all day, pick him up, bathe and feed him, spend QT with him, and going to sleep. During the weekend, it was all about the turn up and having fun. However, I never neglected my mommy duties. I had in-house babysitters, the best you could ask for. I had a few niggas I was busting it open for, but my main nigga was this fine ass fat boy I met off Facebook. His name was DJ Smooth. We spent many nights on the phone together caking. He became my main thing, even came over from time to time and visited me.

DBoy kept insisting that I took my case to trial like he was, but what he failed to realize was that he had money and a lawyer, I was broke and had a public defender. The FED's were already watching us and knew exactly what the fuck was going on. The undercovers had wiretaps on he, and I had to have my levels reviewed so see where I stood and at the time I was going to need to serve. When I started my level was 32, it did not help that the undercover made a statement saying, "She broke it down, weighed it, and collected the money like she has done this many times before." After they included all the factors, my level went down to 20. I finally agreed to sign a plea for six years after my public defender told me that was good, and I needed to accept it. Also signing a plea deal would take my charges from four counts of dealing to two, but the conspiracy would still stick. I had no idea what that six years included, it was all up to the judge and what he felt was necessary. It could have been all six years in prison, or split between work release, home detention and or probation. After signing the plea, I had to wait a few weeks before I went in front of the judge to learn what my punishment was going to be.

Warning Before Destruction

Chapter 24
Losing Myself...the Sentencing

I signed my plea, but my court date was a few weeks away on August 1st. In the meantime, going out and running the streets was not my focus. I started spending more time with my son. Work and home. I had to gather letters from all my family and friends so I could turn them into the judge. Me and DJ Smooth became closer too. He told me he was going to ride out with me every step of the way. He told me he would look out for my son, too. He was a real nigga, and I was happy he was my nigga. Even though I was still fucking with other niggas, he was my main nigga, and I knew it was time for me to go do my time soon so I needed to keep the realest nigga on my team and cut off all the other niggas.

My court date finally arrived. I made sure all my team was there to support me. Cheryl, Brian, Stephanie, Cheleste, Patricia, Mama Latifa, Baba Musa and some of my coworkers. As the judge read all my letters and read my pretrial report I sat there nervous.

"I hope now you have learned a lesson through all of this. You must serve six months in a federal prison, six months in a halfway house and five years' probation." The judge sentenced me. I was sick. I cried as well as Stephanie and Cheleste. It could have been worse but one year away from my son, family and friends wasn't sitting well with me. It was not a womens federal prison close, the closest one was in Alderson, West Virginia.

"I just request I can stay out until after my son's first birthday November 9th?" I pleaded

"You will have to take that up with your probation officer who will get all of that settled for you." The judge told me.

Court ended, but I was still on pretrial reporting to my pretrial officer and doing drops until my probation officer called me and told me it was time to turn myself in. October came around, Mama Latifah and Baba Musa were selling their house. So, me and Cheryl had to find a place to stay.

Cheryl found a 3-bedroom apartment for me, Khari, her baby brother Jah and herself. She told me to stay low key because I was not on her lease and I could be put out. She did not put me on the lease because she knew I was going through this open case.

One day, I decided to have DJ Smooth sneak and see me while she was at work. We sat outside and chilled. Like always he supported me and told me he had my back the whole ride. He made sure he told me every chance he got.

Somebody called the office on me and told Cheryl I had company and I was staying at the apartment. The office called and we were evicted for me living there and not being on the lease. Cheryl was pissed at me. "Now you must find a place to live. I will not let you get me evicted from two places, and you can't get your own place because we don't know the details of when you have to turn yourself in. I am pissed off at you, Rochelle. Now I'm about to have to pay two rents so this doesn't go on my credit." She was pissed. I was upset my damn self because I had no idea where I was about to live at for the next few months with my baby. I had nowhere to go. Now, I was under even more stress from being a single mother, with DBoy being gone, being homeless and going to prison in a few months.

I had a coworker who I was close to, her name was Shanna. She was a little older than me, single with no kids who just bought a huge 5-bedroom house. She was a great support system since I started the Defenders Direct almost 3 years ago. She was nice enough to rent a room out to me so I could have a place to stay for me and Khari until it was time to turn myself in. It was a huge two bedroom and a bathroom connected. She made sure she told me the rules up front, and no company was the main rule. I had no choice but to respect that. I felt bad as fuck for getting Cheryl put out. DJ Smooth was staying with his grandma so staying with him was not an option. He would remind me daily that all this was temporary.

I finally got a call from my probation officer.

"Hello, Rochelle?" He confirmed it was me.

"Yes sir?" I replied.

"Okay, I have the details for you so you can start your time. You are scheduled to be at the gates of Alderson Prison, in Alderson West Virginia no later than 10:00 am on December 29th. Do you have any questions?" he asked.

"No sir." I replied. Even though I was sad it was almost time for me to leave, I was happy it was almost time for me to start this journey and get it over with. I have lost so many things and people in this process. My life was placed on hold and I was ready to start moving forward. I wanted to be the best mother I could be. Cheryl agreed to take care of Khari the year I was away. I was thankful for that because if it wasn't for her, my baby would have been in the system. I had to sign over temporary guardianship to her so she could take care of all his doctor appointments and stuff while I was gone.

Me and Khari's birthday came up. It was his 1st birthday and my 22nd birthday. I made sure he had a nice house party at Shanna's house. It was a nice turn out, he got many gifts. I was overly happy to be there for my baby's 1st birthday. I took plenty of pictures so I could send off to DBoy. My girls Cheleste, Stephanie and Patricia made sure they showed out for my birthday. It was a celebration for my 22nd and a going away party for me. It had been a few months since I went out and had a ball like that. I even hit a blunt a few times. I had to turn myself in soon so fuck pretrial at this point.

Warning Before Destruction

It was a few more weeks before I had to turn myself in. I spent most of that time with Khari, and getting things prepared. I gave my two weeks' notice to my job. I had most of my stuff put away in storage, all it really was clothes. I got all of Khari's things settled and with Cheryl. Celeste was getting her life together. She got a job at my old job Defender. I knew the repo people would eventually come get the truck, because even though she was getting it together she still needed more time before she could take on another bill such as a car note. I asked Shanna if she would file my taxes for me so I could get me a car and have a little bit of money to come home to. As the real ass person she was, she told me she would do that for me. I didn't too much trust Cheryl with my tax money which is why I asked Shanna to handle it for me. All the legal stuff was handled so Cheryl could take care of Khari for me. I had to provide my own transportation to turn myself in. I brought my bus ticket as close to the prison as I could get, then I had to take a taxi one hour away. Through the mountains and to the gates of the prison. I brought myself a fresh pair of Reeboks. Me, Cheleste, and Stephanie had a last girl's night together. We went and got matching tattoos on our chest with hearts and the first initial to our last name. We were locked in for life, I was blessed to have them, they did not give up on me and was ready to ride out with me.

Warning Before Destruction

DBoy called to have the last conversation with me before I took off. He signed a plea to do 10 to 15, but the judge ended up giving him 10 years in prison. Meanwhile, the state picked up the charges for him being a serious violent felony found with a handgun which was inside his safe. Being a serious violent felon with a gun charge was an automatic five years. He was going to court to ask the judge if he could combine the state and fed time, but the judge was not letting up and she was making him serve his time separately. He told me to keep my head up, stay focused, get in and get out.

The time finally came. It was time for me to leave everything in Indianapolis, including my first-born son, and get ready for a new journey which was in a woman's federal prison, which was seven hours away. It was December 28th, I had to leave the day before so I could get there by 10:00AM. Cheryl, Khari, Cheleste and Stephanie all packed up in the car as we headed to the bus station. After our tears and goodbyes, it was time for me to leave. Khari was just turning 1 so he could not understand what was going on. The whole Greyhound ride I just listened to music as my mind was going through a lot of thoughts. Leaving my baby was the hardest part. After a long six hours of riding on the bus, I heard "Next stop is Beckley, West Virginia,"

The black Greyhound driver announced over the speaker. My thoughts were damn, closer and closer to Federal Prison

Alderson. As I got to the last stop it was time for me to get off and catch my taxi another hour away. I was still making good time. As we got closer and closer to the prison, I called Cheryl and Khari to let them know I had made it. The taxi pulled up to the parking lot where I got out. I cried and said a prayer as I hit the button to get in the gate.

"How may we help you?" The country accent came over the intercom.

"Yes, my name is Rochelle Brown and I am here to turn myself in." I said as my voice crackled.

"Okay ma'am. A milk truck will be out to pick you shortly." She said. I turned my phone off and put it in my pocket as the gate opened. I saw the milk truck coming towards me. I walked in the gate as it slammed behind me. Everything that had gotten me to this point replayed in my mind repeatedly. Some of the shit I've done in my life, I have no regrets while some, if I could I'd turn back the hands of time and think twice. Hearing the steel gate slam behind me, I took a deep breath and prepared for my life behind bars for the next six months, and the following six months in work release. Life dealt me a shitty hand, and I played for keeps. This is my story. Sometimes the warning of a storm brewing comes before the destruction, and sometimes there seems to be no warning at all.

THE END....

OR SO I THOUGHT

Warning Before Destruction

ORDER FORM

DIAMANTE' PUBLICATIONS, LLC

2483 Heritage Village 16-341

Snellville, GA 30078

Name (please print):_____

Address:_____

City/State:_____

Zip:_____

QTY	TITLES	PRICE

DO YOU HAVE A LOVED ONE ON LOCK ???

Diamante PUBLICATIONS

Dear Supporter,

I'm sure that we can all agree on one thing: literacy is an important skill that everyone should be allowed to exercise. Whether you're a lover of gritty street drama, erotic enlightenment, or riveting romance, the opportunity to avail yourself of quality reads to sharpen your mind and sate your thirst for literature should always be available to you no matter who you are or where you are.

Diamante' Publications believes in equal opportunity where literacy is concerned. In line with our beliefs, we've developed Diamonds on Lock, a prison book program that provides incarcerated readers with quality reading material monthly at a cheaper rate. By enrolling your imprisoned loved one in this program you are not only supporting literacy but also showing your family member/friend that you love them and you support their interests.

How Does It Work?

Book Selection: Subscribed inmates will receive three (3) Diamante' Publications novels monthly. As your inmate's D.O.L. subscriber, you must visit the Diamonds on Lock webpage monthly to select your inmate's book choices or three (3) novels will be randomly selected by our staff.

Payments: Monthly subscriptions are $25.00 per inmate. Subscription payments must be made online solely via the D.O. L. (Diamante' Publications) website. Subscriptions are pay as you go with no contract holding you to monthly obligations. For each month that you desire for your inmate to receive a shipment, you simply pay the subscription fee for that month. For your inconvenience, you have the choice of also paying for multiple months upfront to ensure that your inmate receives a shipment for each of those months. Book selections will only be sent out upon receipt of payment.

Shipment: Each month your inmate's book selections will be sent directly to them from us. Simply provide us with their complete institution mailing address and inmate number to assure proper delivery.

It's really just that easy. With the click of a button and for only $25.00 per month at your discretion, you can put hot and new releases in the palms of your loved ones hands. We at Diamante' Publications thank you for your interest in maintaining active literacy skills and going above and beyond to support your inmate's reading interests. We look forward to serving you and building a lasting relationship that will enhance the overall literary community.

Sincerely,
Ebonee' Oliver, CEO
Brandon Abby, President

Stay tuned as Diamante' Publications has plenty
more heat for you

Join our mailing list
diamantepublications@gmail.com

To see what's releasing next, read a sneak peek or
win great prizes

YOU CAN ALSO VISIT US AT
www.diamantepublications.com

Please leave us on a Review
@Amazon.com
@Goodreads.com

Made in the USA
Monee, IL
28 February 2020